I SAW WHAT I SAW

A HARMONY NEIGHBORHOOD COZY MYSTERY

TONY GARRITANO

COZY BOOKS

COPYRIGHT PAGE

This is a work of fiction. Names, characters, places, and incidents either are the product of the author's imagination or are used fictitiously. Any resemblance to actual persons, living or dead, events, or locales is entirely coincidental.

Copyright © 2021 by Anthony Garritano

Publisher's Cataloging-in-Publication data

Names: Garritano, Tony, author.

Title: I saw what I saw: a Harmony neighborhood mystery / Tony Garritano.

Series: A Harmony Neighborhood Mystery

Description: Wilton, CT: Cozy Books, 2021.

Identifiers: LCCN: 2021919388 | ISBN: 978-1-7376147-1-5 (hardcover) | 978-1-7376147-0-8 (paperback) | 978-1-7376147-2-2 (ebook)

Subjects: LCSH Journalists--Fiction. | Murder--Fiction. | Mystery fiction. | BISAC FICTION / Mystery & Detective / Cozy / General

Classification: LCC PS3607.A7658 I83 2021 | DDC 813.6--dc23

www.cozybooks.com

❀ Created with Vellum

DEDICATION

This book is a dream come true, but I didn't get here alone. I have a huge support group cheering me on and I owe them everything. I want to thank:

My best friend and wife. A lot of people get married, but few find a true partner and sole mate. I am a very lucky man. I have found it all in you, my wife.

My two sons. Seeing my two sons grow up into the men that they are now has been the greatest gift. With every passing day I grow more and more proud of my two boys.

My mother. I am who I am because of my mother. She has been by my side, and on my side from the very beginning. Through it all, she is there standing with me.

My grandmother. There are few constants in this life. A constant for me is and always has been my Grandmother/Nanny. She is always there telling me that I can do anything that I set my mind to.

My two nieces. Gianna is a shinning star filled with love and talent. Nicalette is a burst of sunshine that lights up every room she walks in.

My brother and sister. Femi is a caring man that has always cared for me. Tina is a spirited woman that always keeps me on my toes.

My mother-in-law. Encouragement is important. My mother-in-law has provided steady encouragement and so much more to me throughout the years.

Kirsten Thompson. It has been a complete joy working with you on the cover design. You are so creative, and you have brought my make-believe world to life visually in ways I could not have imagined.

CHAPTER 1
THE MORNING IT ALL BEGAN

I could feel the tension rising in me. I could feel the sweat starting to form. This was where all the action took place. It was the only closed office on the floor in our newsroom. It was the lair of the editorial director, Duke. Everyone else resided in cubes. Funny how sitting in my little cube felt so much more comfortable than sitting here in this huge corner office. My editor, Charlie, stood next to me, also waiting as Duke read my story. The silence filled the room. Everything was so still; but that was about to change.

"What is this, sweetie?" Duke barked.

My eyes widened at that remark and I leaned forward in my chair. I clenched my fist to hold back the rising rage I felt. Who did he think he was, calling me "sweetie?" How arrogant! How condescending! How sexist! In that moment, I could feel my heart racing. I knew what was about to be said and I braced for the devastation.

"It's the story of the robbery of Annalise Taylor's jewels," I responded politely.

"You call this a story? I call it the second Bible!" Duke bellowed.

"She worked very hard on the story, Duke, and it is very thorough," Charlie said.

My hero. Charlie took a lot of pride in being a mentor and showing the ropes to new people entering the newsroom. He was a counter to Duke in that he was nurturing and supportive. Charlie worked hard to teach you how to tell the story without prejudice or exaggeration. His many years of wisdom could be seen in every wrinkle on his face and every white hair in his beard.

"Ask me if I care if it's thorough! I don't. It's too long. It doesn't grab me," Duke explained gruffly.

"I talked to everyone involved in the case and all of the victim's family members and friends. I literally spent hours with each of them. I feel like I really know Annalise Taylor. I feel like I told her story so people reading it will really know her too," I said.

With that, I pounded my fist on his desk to emphasize how deeply I felt about what I said. Too bad his desk was cluttered with old newspapers. I doubt he could see below my torso with all this mess on his desk. Regardless, I was going to stand my ground. I was not going to let myself be bullied or dismissed. It's hard to put so much of yourself into something as a writer and get all that hard work dismissed and discredited. Well, Duke was not going to get the better of me, no matter what his title was!

"Who cares who Annalise is? I just want to know what happened to her jewels. Everyone in town gushes about those jewels," Duke interrupted.

His face was turning a bright shade of red at this point. His temper was flaring, and he was on a roll. He felt strongly about his opinions, and he wanted me to know it. He was the king of this castle, and nobody stood a chance of unseating him.

"This story is just too much, too much of everything. There are too many quotes. There are too many sources. There is too much backstory."

"I knew you would feel this way, Duke, but she asks a lot of questions, and her questions are usually very good. She really wants to understand her story and its players," Charlie pointed out.

I knew Charlie was proud of my work, but hearing those words come out of his mouth was so satisfying. I took what Charlie taught me about writing and put it into practice in my story, and he appreciated that, a lot.

"I don't care! I just want to finish reading her story before my next birthday!" Duke yelled. "I won't publish this story like this. It's not working!"

"But—" I tried to say. At that point, Charlie looked at me and I knew he was telling me it didn't matter what I said, my story was dead. He didn't have to utter another word; I saw it all in his face. I had to rework it for it to run. Journalism is a hierarchy, and if your editor doesn't like your story, it doesn't run, at least not without heavy edits.

Charlie took my hand and walked me back to my cubicle. He sat me down and stared intently at me. I could tell he was thinking hard about exactly what to say. He leaned in closer and suddenly, his white-and-yellow beard turned into whiskers. His ears darted out of his head to form perfect triangles filled with black, orange, and white fur. He stretched out his hand to touch my shoulder. It was a gentle embrace. I looked down to see it wasn't a hand at all, it was a chunky paw.

I woke up in an instant, pulling off my sleeping mask. As my eyes adjusted to the light coming in from the window, I quickly realized that I wasn't in the newsroom anymore, I was back in my safe, soft bed. It was all a dream—or rather, a nightmare—and there, on my chest, was my calico cat, Majesta. Waking me up at 7:00 a.m. sharp with a big, wet lick across my forehead followed by a head-butt is her thing. She wanted to eat, and she wanted attention. As usual, I gave in to her demands.

I rolled out of bed, brushed my teeth, and went down to the kitchen to feed her. I called my cat Majesta, but I should have called her Pushy Cat or Boss Lady, because that would have been more accurate.

My house was my kingdom, and here, I was queen. I chose to function differently from Duke. I chose to rule with kindness, not fear or intimidation. I walked down the stairs, enjoying the warmth from the cream-colored carpet. I knew every inch of this house; after all, I grew up here. Unfortunately, I was the only one in the family left living here, but the others came back to visit, as we were very close.

Working in that newsroom had been a low point in my life, but in the end, I was grateful for knowing both Charlie and Duke, because they taught me a lot about me. You could learn a lot about yourself by how you relate to others, and by how they relate to you. I had some good times in that newsroom, even if I was never given my dream stories to cover, and the stories I did cover were often criticized. Eventually, all the insults became too much for me and I had to go my own way. It wasn't an easy decision for me to leave, but things were getting too tense, and I needed more freedom. I couldn't continue to let Duke stop me from practicing my form of journalism.

Freedom is a tricky thing; it means different things to different people. I almost tripped from Majesta rubbing against my leg. Clearly, my freedom was still limited. Majesta's needs had to be met. As I cracked open her can of cat food, I looked out the kitchen window into the morning sky. It was so blue and warm and welcoming. Life on my cul-de-sac was as close to perfect as you could get. Funny how unaware I was that this wasn't going to be a routine morning. You see, this was not today's morning routine, this was what happened yesterday. Today was a very different day, in more ways than one.

Looking back at what happened yesterday, I had no idea how much my perspective on life was going to change. It was going to be a doozy of a day. As a former crime reporter, I paid close attention to the details, even what may seem like small and insignificant details to people like Duke. You never know what's going to break a story wide open. However, I could never have imagined becoming part of the story. It was one thing to see something on television or to read about something in a newspaper or magazine, but when you witness it happening firsthand, it just takes on new meaning. But let's not get ahead of ourselves.

The day was off to a great start. I was in a good mood after feeding Majesta and getting ready for my day to begin. I was a woman on a mission. In that moment, I was ready for the next step in my usual morning routine, getting a real bagel at Harry's Bagel Shop. Harry's looked like a diner out of the 1950s, and when you stepped in the front door, you felt transported back to a simpler time, when your neighbors were not just neighbors, they were friends.

I got my jeans on quick, threw on a shirt and I was out the door. Sheila Sammartino was on her way to get her favorite fresh bagel and hot, black coffee. Yes, I sometimes talk about myself in the third person. In my opinion, it's a cute quirk, even though I was teased mercilessly in high school for doing it. Sometimes you just have to be you, regardless of what others say. I was quirky and I knew it.

I got in my RAV4 and I was ready to go. I checked my mirrors, popped in a CD, stepped on the brake, shifted my car into reverse, and I was rolling down my driveway into the street of my tiny cul-de-sac.

When they say home is where the heart is, they are not lying. Everyone knew each other on my cul-de-sac, and we all got along. It was perfect. I waved at my neighbor Sam. Sometimes we would talk on my way to Harry's, but today I just wanted that fresh, hot bagel. I could taste it, and soon it was going to be all mine.

But that had to wait, because something big was about to happen. I can't believe I did this, but I did, and I felt so stupid afterward for it, but not-so-great things happen in life all the time, I guess. Nobody is perfect. I'm just glad nobody got hurt; at least not this time.

CHAPTER 2
OUR FIRST ENCOUNTER

I could smell the fresh bread in the air. It was calling to my senses. Some people have to have their morning coffee, well, I had to have my morning bagel from Harry's. It's like I'm in a trance or something until I taste that first bite of fresh bread covered in homemade cream cheese like only Harry can make it. In fact, I was so distracted, I really wasn't paying attention to where I was going. You know how that is? In that moment, I felt the collision of steel on steel and I thrust forward sharply before hitting my brakes.

What did I do? I crashed my car right into a small moving van that was trying to get into the house next door. Luckily, I was going slow at the time of the accident, and so was he, but when my car hit his van, I was still startled, and the jolt shocked me.

I know you're wondering right about now if this is the thing that would change my perspective on life that I mentioned earlier. Nope. That event is still to come, but this situation that I found myself in was quite impactful, pardon the pun; it was just not the perspective-changing event that was yet to happen.

"I am so sorry," I said as I walked over to the front of the van. "I can't believe I did this. I am so ashamed."

The man was on his cell phone. He was texting away. I just hit his van and he's texting. I thought to myself: this is why there are texting while driving laws in this country. Nobody these days can live without texting. It's crazy! It's infuriating, actually!

"Are you okay?" I yelled. "Are you okay?" I began frantically circling the van, looking for any visible dent. Luckily, I didn't see anything. It was just a fender bender, thank God!

"Why are you screaming?" the man asked. His voice sounded calm, and not the least bit angry. In fact, his voice had a soothing quality to it; or maybe it just soothed me to hear a voice that wasn't full of hate. Maybe *hate* is a strong word, but when you get in a car accident, you're often filled with hate for the other guy. At least I am.

"Why aren't you responding to me?" I yelled.

"You certainly have a flair for the dramatic, which I appreciate. I like a woman that can make a great entrance. Wait, you are the one that hit me and now you're yelling at *me*?" he questioned. He stared intently at my face.

"I'm so sorry," I responded, again feeling so ashamed of what I did.

Now we were looking face-to-face and I could see him. He was adorable! Think Regé-Jean Page, but cuter. He looked to be about my age, with caramel skin, big, brown eyes, and dark, curly hair. I hate square jaws and distinct cheekbones. He was not that way at all. His looks, dare I say, were perfect. Not that I'm so superficial that all I pay attention to are a person's looks, but when something is staring you in the face that's so amazing, it's hard to ignore. Speaking of staring, he was still staring at my face.

"My name is Reginald, but everyone calls me Reggie. By the looks of things, we are about to be neighbors." I tried not to laugh. Who names their child Reginald these days? I held it together. I had already made a complete fool of myself hitting his van and yelling at him; I wasn't going to be caught laughing at the man's name too.

Then, the gravity of my situation sank in: oh my God, I just hit my new neighbor. How embarrassing! *I need to change the subject and free myself of this humiliation.*

"So it's a sunny day today," I said. How dumb. Why would he care about the weather when his van just got hit by his new neighbor's car?

"Dimples," he responded.

"What did you say? Are you okay?" I couldn't help but stare into his sweet, chocolate-brown eyes. I hoped he didn't notice too much.

"Yes, I'm fine. Your dimples are beautiful."

"Are you serious? I don't have dimples."

"Yes, you do. Smile."

This was becoming very weird. Nonetheless, I smiled, and shortly after I smiled, so did he.

"There they are," he said joyfully. "I'm going to call you Dimples."

"What? Nobody has ever noticed my dimples before. Let's get back to the topic at hand. I do apologize. How did you find out about this house and our little cul-de-sac?"

"I've noticed your dimples. They're beautiful. In terms of this house, my realtor showed me the place and I fell in love. I also think it's so appropriate that they call this town Harmony. It's so quaint. It's a wonderful little neighborhood. Harmony is just a perfect name for a town, in my opinion. All great love stories have the lovers falling in love at first sight. For now, this house is the woman of my dreams."

"I know what you mean." As he talked, I looked closer and closer at him, and I could understand him. Wait, I don't want him to think I meant that I was in love with him. "I mean, I love the houses here, not you, the houses." Way to go, Sheila; that cleared it up. This just was not going well at all. So what did I do to turn the corner on this horrible conversation? I kept asking more questions, of course. "Are you new to this area entirely? I mean, to this town and state?"

"I am new to the town, but not the state. You ask a lot of questions, Dimples," Reggie remarked, and smiled. He was obviously humoring me.

"I hear that a lot. It's an occupational hazard, I guess. What do you do?"

"Another question. You just can't help yourself. I'm a theatre reporter. How about you?" He looked down after declaring his profession. I guess he wasn't too comfortable with it for some reason. I wondered why.

"That makes perfect sense. I was a crime reporter. Now I have my own online publishing company. I blog. How did you get into theater?"

"Another great question," Reggie laughed. "I've always loved theater, but becoming a theater reporter was not really my choice; it was the first job I got after failing as an actor. If you're not friends with Tyler Perry, it can be hard to get a good role as a Black man. Hollywood is looking for the next George Clooney or Brad Pitt, not the next Sydney Poitier or Denzel Washington. That's just the sad truth."

If I hadn't just hit his car, I could swear we were meant to be neighbors. We're two people who both feel marginalized by our society trying to make our own success story happen. Having another writer on the block to talk to would have been great if I didn't almost kill him with my car. How could we get close now? He probably hates me.

"I'm fine, Dimples. I'm not hurt at all. And don't worry, I don't hate you," Reggie said calmly and in a reassuring tone.

Wow, now he was reading my mind! The calling me Dimples thing was weird, but I let it slide. He knew what I needed to hear. He knew how to free me of the guilt I felt for hitting his moving van. He was too good to be true, for sure.

"That's great," I said with a smile. Oops, I didn't want him to think I was happy about this situation. "I mean it's great that you are okay, it's not great that I hit your van."

"I know what you meant," he said while laughing again.

Now he laughed at me again. He must have thought I was so flighty. He must have thought I was a real flake. There was no coming back from this for me.

"I don't think ill of you or that you're flighty, Dimples. You probably were just in a hurry to get somewhere very important," Reggie noted.

There he went again, reading my mind and knowing exactly how to respond to me. Maybe there was hope for me getting out of this with my integrity. "Great, but I didn't think that you thought I was a flake. I don't know what I thought exactly, but I surely didn't think that. Why would you? I mean, besides the whole me hitting you with my car thing."

"Of course. Well, I am going to finish pulling in my new driveway and start moving into my new house," Reggie reported. "See you soon," he concluded as he started to drive further into his driveway. I waved at him to stop, and he did.

"One more tiny question," I said. "You will stop by once you're settled, right? I mean, because we're neighbors now."

He nodded his head and that was that. Well, that went well, I thought. I guess it wasn't too horrible. He didn't seem to hate me or think I was a flake. Or did he? Maybe he just said those things to get away from me. Who knows?

At the time, I didn't know what a great team we would become.

Either way, I was a woman on a mission, and I wasn't about to let this car accident stop me from my goal of getting that hot, fresh bagel from Harry's. Once I had that bagel, things would settle down and life would be normal again—so I thought. At least I wouldn't go around running into neighbors with my car anymore. I must admit, looking back, it might have been a weird first meeting, but I was glad to meet Reggie, and glad he would be my new neighbor.

As for hoping things would soon go back to normal, well, that just wasn't going to happen anytime soon.

CHAPTER 3
A SAFE PLACE, FOR ME AT LEAST

Harry's Bagel Shop has always been a second home for me. Everyone has a safe place, or at least, they should. You need a place where you can unwind with your peers. You need to be among your people. There is a freeing feeling associated with meeting friends at a local hangout. It's good to get out into the world and socialize.

I'm not sure people think of a deli as a second home or a safe place, but that's what Harry's was, and still is, for me, and pretty much everyone in our neighborhood. The minute you walk in the door it's like walking back in time. The deli looks just like a 1950s diner. It has lots of silver chrome stools lining a long counter that spans the entire length of the deli. The floor has a black-and-white checkered pattern and the booths across the wall are all bright and pastel-colored. Everyone in our neighborhood gathers at Harry's, and everyone in Harmony knows everyone.

"It's my friend Sheila!" Harry said with a big smile. He came out from behind the counter and gave me a huge hug.

"Harry, you are not going to believe what happened to me."

"Tell me all about it."

"I was so distracted by the desire to get your bagels that I hit my new neighbor with my car."

"Are you serious? Was everyone okay?"

"Yes, but I am mortified about it. How do I talk to him again?"

"As long as everyone is okay, that's all that really matters. Here, I'll give you your usual on the house this morning."

"You are the best, Harry."

"I always like to help my friends. Never forget those that stand by you, that's what I always say."

Harry was just amazing. He always knew how to cheer me up. And I was going to call on him for help real soon, and he would literally swing into action. He was a short, chubby, happy guy with a bald head and a thick, white mustache. Meeting Harry was a real blessing in my life.

I remember the first day I met Harry very vividly. After Duke decided not to publish my first story in its original form, I was down that day. I felt defeated. Charlie took me into his office and he told me not to let Duke stop me from pursuing the story and getting it published. Charlie told me we all have a boss to report to and we must know how to get our stories out the best way we can.

In a lot of ways, that first story that Duke criticized was like a baby to me. I birthed it and, when I sent it over for copy editing, I thought it was perfect. I guess everyone thinks their child is perfect. Charlie taught me about how important my audience was. As a reporter, you can't always write for yourself. Your story must get past several layers of editing and several editors before it goes to print. From there it goes into the world for people to consume, people who will, hopefully, love reading it just as much as you loved writing it.

It's both freeing and nerve-racking when you finally get that story published. I always second-guess things. I think to myself, did I do a good job telling that story? Did I cover every angle? Will the reader respond to it?

Despite Charlie's words of encouragement, I was second-guessing myself that day, so I decided to get out of the office and take a little walk. Walking has always been a way for me to reflect. That day I was deep in thought and again I ran into someone, just not with my car this time.

Harry was sweeping outside his deli and I was thinking about my story and not paying attention to what was in front of me. I walked into him, and that's how we met for the very first time. He was new in town, and anytime anyone is new in Harmony, that's a big deal. We all just had to know each other. You know how it is in small towns, right?

Anyway, after the collision, he invited me into his deli. It was empty, so he sat down with me and we talked. It was a great conversation. He, too, reassured me that I was on the right track with my story and my choice of careers, I just had to keep moving forward in a positive direction so I could get my story out there. I had to make adjustments so Duke would publish it, and learn from Duke's criticism so I knew the type of story he would publish going forward.

I guess everyone encounters that person at their work that rubs them the wrong way. So what do you do? In this case, you find a way to deal with it in such a way that everyone wins. I had to keep digging and interviewing sources to produce the best story I could, but it also had to adhere to a strict word count and include the appropriate hooks to really move the reader. In the end, I figured out after talking with Harry that wasn't such a bad thing.

It's experiences like meeting someone like Harry that shape a person. It's great to meet a positive person to counteract the less friendly people. I wish I had that as a little girl growing up. When I was a little girl, my father left abruptly. There was no explanation, and I never saw him again. I always wondered why he left and how I could get him back. The experience left me with so many questions and a longing to get answers and fix things. In a lot of ways, Harry was that father figure I could talk to and turn to who would never leave me. He would always be there.

"Are you okay now, Sheila?" Harry asked after he handed me my usual bagel and coffee.

"I'm fine now," I said.

"Good, now go join your friends over there." He pointed to a table with four people sitting at it, all looking up at me. These were my people. This was my breakfast club, of sorts. We were regulars that always came to Harry's for breakfast and sat together to start our day as a group.

In a way, I guess Harry was my father in that moment, making sure I was okay before he sent me off on the bus to school so I could meet up with my friends. So I left Harry's presence and walked over to my friends, as a good daughter should. Of course, I didn't realize how much this "good daughter" was going to need her "father" shortly, but Harry would not disappoint. He would help me once called upon.

CHAPTER 4
THE CALM BEFORE THE STORM

Seeing my friends waiting for me at the table at Harry's was so comforting. We were a great team. We would meet almost every morning over a bagel, and all was right with the world. After my first conversation with Harry, I started coming to the deli before work each morning. It was a habit. One morning, I saw two people sitting near the window in the front of the deli, a man and a woman. They were arguing. Of course, I was curious as to what all the commotion was about. I couldn't just let it go, so I walked over.

The fight seemed intense. I thought I would be breaking up a domestic squabble. Boy, was I wrong. Samantha and Oliver were not a married couple at all. Samantha was skinny, had long, black hair and wore huge, black glasses that seemed to be the size of half her face. She was the president of our local bank. Oliver had red hair and was filled with freckles. His personality was as fiery as his carrot-top locks, which was very appropriate given that he was our neighborhood fire chief.

"Everyone knows that Wonder Woman is the best!" Samantha yelled.

"Please, Captain America all the way!" Oliver responded.

Yup, they were arguing about comic book superheroes. Samantha loved DC and Oliver was a Marvel fan. The conversation shocked me at first, but I didn't let that deter me, as I am a very determined person.

"Is this really worth fighting over?" I interrupted.

That was a mistake because, in that moment, they both turned on me. I have been schooled about different superheroes ever since. At that point, we became a gang of three.

A few months later, Clark joined our group. Clark was an English teacher. He loved teaching. He, too, got involved because he overheard Samantha and Oliver discussing superheroes as I just sat quietly and listened along that day. I think the conversation reminded him of something he would hear his students discussing, and he was intrigued.

"Excuse me, may I join your conversation?" he asked.

Of course, we let him sit with us. At that point, he began a full-throated defense of the 1960s *Batman* TV series. I was stunned how this distinguished-looking, well-groomed Asian man could fit in so nicely with the quirky, comic-book-loving couple. Now we were a group of four.

Our last member was Leslie. She was a blonde who always wore clothes that looked a little too small for her and showed a little too much skin. She was our mayor's secretary. One day she "accidentally" spilled her coffee in Clark's lap. She was very apologetic, and has always been very sympathetic to anything that came out of Clark's mouth.

So that's our morning group for you. Each of us different, but we seem to fit nicely together. I often ran stories by the group. I used them as a sounding board, of sorts, and it worked. I learned so much and saw things in many different ways after talking to them. They opened my eyes about so many things over the years. Yesterday, I was eager to talk about human relationships. I was still thinking about Reggie and how I could restart that association.

"How important is your first meeting?" I asked.

"You mean how important is your first encounter with a person in determining your future relationship with that person?" Clark asked.

"There Sheila goes again, starting a conversation with a question," Samantha said.

"I think first meetings are very important and should be planned well," noted Leslie as she gazed into Clark's eyes.

Being a man, Clark was oblivious to the real meaning behind Leslie's comment. "I think it can be important, but not always. I started off not really liking our vice principal, but now that has changed."

"I'm sure your vice principal is a very nice man," Leslie added.

"Actually, our vice principal is a woman," Clark said.

"I'm sure," Leslie remarked, then she abruptly got up to refill her coffee.

"I'm serious. I got off to a bad start with my new neighbor and I'd like to make it right," I said. "What should I do?"

"You should look for his weakness and go for that," Oliver said. "The best heroes find the villain's weakness and exploit it."

"I don't want to exploit him, and I don't see him as a villain either," I responded.

"I didn't mean it literally. The villain is the obstacle in the story that the hero must overcome, just like your obstacle of a not-so-great introduction is in this case. Go over to him and feel him out. Find out what makes him tick, and the more you know, the more you can appeal to him."

"That's sound advice, but how do I break the ice?"

"Do what you do best, ask a question," Oliver retorted.

"I guess you are right."

"It doesn't happen often, but he's right this time around," added Samantha. "I think you have to have a question or two in your head and go over to his house armed with a conversation starter. It'll work. You'll see."

See what I mean? They always challenge me to think about things differently. Being among this group of five has helped me so much through the years, and that was not going to change. During the next few very dramatic minutes, I would need all they had to offer to get me through what was about to happen. You never know how important your friends are until you go through something devastating and they are there to calm you down and provide real perspective. When it comes to matters of life and death, perspective can make all the difference.

CHAPTER 5
A TRAGEDY OCCURS

O ur conversation switched to politics, one of the dreaded topics. The saying goes that you should always steer clear of discussing politics and religion. However, Harry had the television on, and the news was discussing the forthcoming election. We were in an election year, and it was a big deal for our town of Harmony because our district attorney, Clarence Wright, was running for governor. He was a traditional Republican running on a campaign based on law and order and, above all else, family values. You either loved him or hated him.

I was in the unique position of having known him a little bit given my past as a crime reporter. I thought he was a good man at his core, but he was obsessed with appearances. During my first interview with him, he spent more time talking about the latest additions to his office than he did about the robbery I was covering at the time.

"What do you think about Clarence?" I asked.

"He's a typical politician," Samantha responded.

"I think it's best not to ask about politics," Clark said.

"I don't know how I feel about him," a man said behind me. I turned around to see an African-American man, probably in his thirties, dressed in a formal suit and tie looking at the television. He obviously heard our conversation and wanted to join, so I thought, but I was wrong. His cell phone rang and he retreated to a chair with his back to us. He was new to town. None of us had seen him before, which meant we all had to know more about him. I wish I wasn't so curious and nosey, but we are who we are.

"It's not going to happen," the man said to whomever he was talking to on his phone. "I will take care of everything, dear. Don't worry about it, dear. It's going to be just fine. Everything will work out. We are meant to be together. I can't move forward on my own without you. Besides, after this meeting, you are going to be so proud to stay my wife. I have a new business deal in the works and it's going to rekindle our relationship when it succeeds. You'll see. You'll stay."

He hung up on that person and got his food. He ordered a bagel and coffee, my usual, which just made me want to know him more. I always get myself into trouble, but that was going to be an understatement in this case.

He got another call, this time from his mother. "Hi, Mom," he said happily. "I know you've been upset recently, but it's all going to turn around. I have a plan. It's going to be big. I know you don't approve, but trust me, it's going to be great!"

This guy was obviously dealing with a lot. At that point his phone rang again, but this call was different. It was weird. "What do you mean?" he asked. "What are you talking about? Are you serious? Remember, this is where you wanted to meet, bro. Okay, I'll see you next door instead."

He was annoyed and he ran out of the deli in a rush. Any normal person would have left well enough alone, but not me. I had to eavesdrop on his conversations. I had to get up the nerve to follow him out of the deli.

I excused myself from the conversation about politics and left the deli after him. I didn't leave immediately, so when I looked both ways after exiting, I didn't see him. Actually, there was nobody at all on the sidewalk. I did see a police car parked a bit further down the block, but nobody was inside.

Then, the yelling started. It was the new guy. It was him. He was in pain. He was getting attacked or beaten or something.

I followed the cries and started to run down the block toward them. I had to help him! As I walked faster, I passed the alley between Harry's and the next group of shops when I heard a garbage can moving toward me and a big thud. That thud was the sound of the man's body hitting the ground in that alley. I quickly turned to look down the alley and what I saw was horrific.

The man was on the ground, screaming that he couldn't breathe as he was assaulted by two police officers: a man and a woman. The male police officer had his knee on the man's neck and the female police officer had her knee on the man's back. I couldn't believe what I was seeing. How could this be happening here, in our little neighborhood of Harmony, right in front of me?

Nobody could see me, and I couldn't really see them, at least not from the front. Their backs were facing me. The woman had pink-tipped platinum hair though, I could see that. Then light flashed in my eyes, and I was blinded. I closed my eyes quickly and reopened them. It was in that moment that I realized that the woman was wearing a gold charm bracelet with tons of hearts on it. The bracelet must have hit the sun and shot the light in my eyes.

I screamed, "STOP!"

In that moment, the policeman turned to face me. I ran away to get help, so I didn't really see him. I don't think he really saw me either; at least, I hope he didn't. I just noticed that he had a long, brown beard and one of his eyes was a cloudy, gray color.

I ran back to Harry's. "Help! The police are killing an innocent Black man!" I yelled.

Harry responded immediately. He got a bat that I guess he kept behind his counter to fend off criminals. "The police are at it again! Not in my town!"

By the time Harry and I quickly ran back to that alley, the two police were gone. I looked across the street only to see that the police car was also gone. I looked back to see Oliver, Samantha, and Clark running toward me.

"I called 9-1-1!" Samantha yelled.

"We're going to get through this," said Clark.

I thought to myself: are we going to get through this? What is the state of the country when something like this can happen in my small neighborhood? How could this be happening? I knelt down over the body of the man I saw those police officers attacking. He didn't have a pulse. He was dead.

CHAPTER 6
THE INQUISITION

I was brought to the police station to give my statement. The irony was not lost on me. I had been in the police station a lot in my day. As a crime reporter, this place became a common stomping ground for me. I was a regular. It had been a while since I was here, but the minute you step into that building, you know exactly where you are and how serious the situation is.

I took my job as a crime reporter very seriously. It was like a calling. I was on a mission when I got a story to track down. I was relentless. I wasn't going to be dismissed or disgraced or disregarded. I knew what I was doing was important and I tried to treat my job with the dignity I felt it deserved. I was proud to be a crime reporter.

Yesterday was a little bit different because I was the one on the receiving end of the questions, but that was okay with me. Of course, I wasn't going to just sit back and answer those questions without asking a few of my own.

"It's been a long time, Lieutenant Crooks. Did you miss me?"

"Actually, no," he smirked. I never got along with this man. Anytime I see him, I smile, because his last name is just too fitting, in my opinion. He was old-school. I don't think he felt comfortable getting grilled by a woman. I observed him calling other women names like honey or doll, but he never called me those names. He did use other not-so-flattering adjectives to describe me from time to time, though.

"So you say two police officers did this?"

"Yes, a man and a woman. I didn't see the woman's face, but she had platinum hair with pink tips. I saw the man's face briefly. All I could make out was his beard and the color of his eyes."

"Well, aren't you helpful," Crooks said sarcastically. "Can you tell me anything that will actually help me identify these two aside from their hair color and facial hair?"

"The last time I checked, I am the one that witnessed a murder; I didn't commit the murder."

"Did anyone else see this murder?"

"I don't think so. The sidewalk was clear at the time I witnessed the attack."

"Did anyone else see these two police officers?"

"I don't think so, as I said, I think the sidewalk was clear. It was early in the morning. Isn't it your job to find witnesses?"

"I know what my job is, thank you."

"Are you trying to say I made this up? That I am lying?"

"Those are your words, not mine. And please, let me ask the questions. You say that you noticed a police car parked nearby. Did you get the license plate number?"

"I did not. I was a little distracted at the time. My mind was elsewhere. I was paying closer attention to the man that your police officers were killing."

"So you say."

I was obviously getting nowhere with this. I was talking to the wrong person. I wasn't being taken seriously. This flunky was not going to listen to me without video footage in hand or a corroborating witness. Trying to convince this guy was a waste of my time. I needed to be free of this conversation as quickly as possible so I could seek greener pastures, so to speak. I told Crooks that I didn't think I could tell him anything further but that I would be sure to get in touch with him if I remembered anything new. He was happy to see me go, and I was happy to depart from his desk, but he couldn't resist one final insult.

"This whole thing is very ironic," he said.

"How do you mean?" I asked.

"Back in the day, you always wanted to cover a murder, if I remember correctly, and now you say you've witnessed one," he smirked.

"I think you are mistaking the word *irony* with the word *tragedy*," I replied, just as I left his desk.

But just because I was leaving his desk did not mean I was about to leave the police station entirely. I knew what I saw, and I was going to tell my story to someone who would really listen to me.

I walked the halls looking for Anthony. He was a cute Italian guy with curly, brown hair. Anytime I needed help with a story, he was always there for me. He was a sergeant at the time I left my job reporting on crime.

I found Anthony talking to a skinny blonde at the watercooler. I waited for her to leave before I approached. He hadn't changed a bit. He looked the same as I remembered him in my mind and, as I would find out, he acted the same as well.

"I heard about what happened," he said.

"It was horrible," I said.

"Crooks is not going to do anything with it."

"I know, that's why I came looking for you. Will you help me here? This can't go unpunished."

"When you're talking about the police investigating a fellow police officer, things get very tricky. You know how these things go. We have never had a 'bad' cop here, and I'm sure everyone wants to keep it that way. We don't want to be the next location inundated by protesters and the like. Plus, it's an election year, and Clarence is running for governor."

"I know, I know, but you can't let this go, can you?" I looked directly into his eyes and I saw that he was sympathetic. He understood where I was coming from, and I knew he would help me get this man some justice. Anthony always had a strong sense of right and wrong, which made talking to him very easy for me. We had a similar worldview in most cases.

"Okay, I'll look into things and I'll keep you informed about what's going on. I'm assuming you won't be hearing from our friend Crooks anymore. He wants this to go away, and my guess is he's going to brush this under the rug."

This couldn't be brushed under the rug. This sort of thing was becoming all too common now, and people were not going to stand for it anymore. The times had changed. Police were no longer above the law, at least when you caught them on video. Too bad I didn't have a video. No matter, this investigation wasn't going to be cut short, not while I was on the case anyway, and now I was on the case.

CHAPTER 7
THE MORNING SCARE

I didn't sleep at all. Who could sleep after such a day? Yesterday was a life-changing day, for sure, but what was I going to do today? That was the question. Was I going to pursue this murder or leave it to the police?

After I left the police station yesterday, I was determined to stay engaged, but today seems different. I am doubting myself today. Do I have what it takes to solve a murder instead of just dreaming of reporting on one? I know I saw two police officers do this, but taking on the police seems so daunting today for some reason.

See what I mean about how often I ask questions? I even ask myself questions a lot. I can't help myself. This was a new day that called for new thinking, or at least rethinking.

Just then, I felt something brush up against my arm. I jumped out of bed. It was just my cat, Majesta. What a fool I am to be afraid of my own cat. It is 7:00 a.m. and, after yesterday, I guess I have a right to be a bit jumpy.

No matter how jumpy I was, I can only imagine how the good police officers must feel. I trust the police, for the most part. I've worked closely with them. I don't have to worry about a police officer misjudging me or projecting their racial stereotypes on me. I'm safe. I'm not a Black person in America.

In the end, no matter how much changes, I guess certain things remain the same. For example, Majesta still needed her breakfast. So I put on my slippers and my housecoat and walked downstairs to the kitchen. My simple, two-story house is quite nice, if I do say so myself, although it is a bit big for just me and Majesta. The main floor has a sitting room, kitchen, TV room, office, and one bathroom. The second floor has three bedrooms and two bathrooms. I keep it tidy and organized at all times. Everything has its place. I am not a clean freak, but I like to know where everything is. When I want something, there should be no question in my mind where I need to go to get it.

Should I do my usual and go to Harry's this morning? I don't know. Everyone is going to be doting on me. They are going to treat me like some helpless damsel in distress that needs comforting or protecting. I am no damsel in distress. I am a strong, independent woman that answers to no one.

I felt something brush up against my arm from on top of the kitchen countertop. It was Majesta again. I wasn't going to jump and let my own cat scare me twice in the same morning. She purred and purred. She always purred when she wanted something, and she would look at me as she did it. Another big purr came out of her tiny mouth as those big, green eyes looked up at me. I looked back at her and the two of us were having a distinct conversation in my head.

"You still have not fed me," she scolded.

"I'm getting to it," I answered.

"You know I don't like to wait."

"I know, I know. It's coming."

Maybe I am not as independent as I think I am. I guess I do answer to some; at least I answer to Majesta anyway. I emptied her food into her bowl on the white quartz island in my kitchen. At that moment, she sprang into action. She jumped from the countertop to the island and started eating away before I had a chance to put the bowl on the floor.

"Don't judge me, I'm hungry," she said.

"I'm not judging you, Majesta, but you could be a bit more

patient," I said. At that moment, I laughed and thought,: she probably gets that lack of patience from me.

Yesterday I witnessed a murder, and today I am having a conversation with my cat. What's next?

A loud bang came from the back of the house. That was not Majesta; she was here with me still gleefully eating away. Somebody fell down. Somebody else was in my house and fell down as they entered through the back door.

This can't be happening. Our cul-de-sac is small and quiet and safe. What should I do? I must fight. I grabbed the broom from the broom closet in the kitchen and slowly walked to the back of the house. I walked quietly. My floors were all hardwood. I didn't want them to creak.

Thankfully, my house is small. I was ready. I was not going to go down without a fight. I was ready to pounce, just like Majesta would if there was a mouse intruder. I could hear the person getting up. I could hear the floor creaking as they walked. The footsteps were getting louder and closer. The person was right around the corner from me. Now was the time for me to strike.

As the person came around the corner, I swung my broom fiercely. I hit him. I swung again and hit him again. I was winning! I was awesome! The person fell to the ground when I realized it was not a man at all, but rather, a woman. She had curly, brownish-red hair and was very well-dressed. Wait, it was Tania, my copy editor and best friend. *What have I done? I killed my best friend!* Okay, I didn't kill her, but I hit her hard with my broom, surely.

I quickly stretched out my hand and helped her up. She was just dazed.

"What the hell are you doing?" Tania yelled.

"Me? You're the one breaking into my house first thing in the morning!" I yelled back.

"I wasn't breaking into your house. I rang the doorbell several times, but you didn't answer. I know you go to Harry's early each morning, so I thought I would stop by and go with you this morning. When you didn't answer, I went around back."

"And you broke in my back door?"

"No, your back door was unlocked, so I let myself in. I was worried. It's not like you to leave the back door unlocked. But once I got in the house, I tripped on your shoes and fell down. That worried me even more because you usually don't leave your shoes lying about either."

"Okay, okay. I get your point," I said. "Yesterday was a tough day. I didn't want to talk to anyone, so when I got home, I entered through the back door to avoid the neighbors. I must have forgotten to lock the door behind me."

"But why didn't you hear the doorbell?"

"I was talking to Majesta. I didn't hear the doorbell."

"Oh, I see. Did Majesta talk back?" Tania asked sarcastically.

"In fact, she did. She wanted her breakfast," I responded equally as sarcastically.

Tania piped down. She could tell I was not myself. She also knew I loved my morning coffee, so she started brewing me a fresh pot.

We met in college. She was my roommate sophomore year. We've been friends ever since. I always think of her as exotic and sophisticated. She is exciting to be around. She always has a fresh idea and a get-up-and-go attitude. She is a doer.

We left the kitchen with our coffee and went to the TV room together. I had a big leather sectional, so it was great to lounge on. Majesta joined us. It was going to be just us three girls chitchatting away.

"Yesterday, I went to Harry's, as usual. Everything was fine until this man entered the shop. He caught my eye."

"That's not a bad thing. Did you get his number?" Tania asked.

"Be serious!" I responded. "He was murdered, and I saw the whole thing."

"Oh my God! That's horrible! What did you do?"

"I ran back to Harry's to get help. By the time we got back to the alley, the murderers were gone and the man was dead."

"What do you mean murderers?"

"There were two people, a man and a woman. The man was choking him on the ground while the woman was holding him down."

29

"That's horrible and frightening. I don't know what I would have done if I were in your shoes. So, what did you do?"

"That's it. The police arrived and took me back to the station to give a statement."

"What police?"

"It was Crooks."

"That ass. On top of seeing a murder, you had to deal with him too. You poor thing."

I told Tania most things. She knew about Charlie and Duke and Crooks and Anthony. Friends talk, and, boy, were we friends, and, boy, did we talk. One night in college, Tania came back late. I knew she was with someone. We talked the rest of that night and into the morning. I missed my first class. It's good to have someone you can really talk to. Everyone needs someone like that in their life.

"So how are you?" Tonia asked.

"What?"

"How are you? You saw a man killed in an alley."

"So?"

"Have you stopped to process everything that happened to you yet?"

I guess I hadn't. I was thinking first about what happened and second about how to solve the situation, but I never stopped to think about how it made me feel. How did it make me feel? That man died and I saw most of it happen. I was there for his final moments of life. How did that make me feel? I felt a tear run down my face, and then more and more. I was crying. I felt so lost. I felt so helpless. I couldn't help him. I couldn't save him. Those two police officers killed him, and I couldn't do anything about it.

Tania pulled me close for a hug. Now she was crying too. "There's nothing you could have done," she said. "You did the right thing. You got help. You are a hero."

"What?" I said. "I am not a hero. He died. I didn't save him. They killed him."

"You did your best. You tried."

I guess Tania was right about that, but my best wasn't good enough. Now I was convinced. I had to do more. I had to get that man justice. I couldn't let them just kill him. Furthermore, if they killed him, they'd kill others.

"So what aren't you telling me?" Tania asked.

We knew each other well. I dried my eyes and looked straight in her face. I had to tell her everything. "The two murderers were police officers."

"Oh my God! Did you recognize them from your days as a crime reporter?"

"No, the woman's back was to me, so I didn't see her. All I saw was that she had platinum hair with pink tips and she wore a gold bracelet with heart charms. I saw the man's face for a second. He had a big beard, and his eyes were different colors. One of his eyes seemed gray and cloudy to me. When I heard you in the back of the house, I thought for a second it might be him. What if he recognized me? What if he knows who I am?"

"We'll get through this," said Tania. "Anything else?"

"Yes, the man was a Black man. He was only out there for a few minutes. He got a strange call and left Harry's. I followed him shortly after he left. There is just no way he had enough time to do anything illegal that would warrant a beating. They targeted him. They must have known him and called him on his phone to draw him out of Harry's. But why would they do that?"

"Who knows? The world is falling apart these days," Tania noted.

Just then, there was a loud noise in the kitchen. It sounded like the window breaking. I jumped to my feet and so did Tania. I still had the broom, and she had the coffee pot still partially filled with the coffee she made for me. We held our weapons tight, screamed out a loud battle cry, and ran in the kitchen ready to fight. We were not going to let those crooked cops get us too. It was not going to happen again. They were not going to murder us.

CHAPTER 8
ASSEMBLING THE TEAM

Tania and I ran into the kitchen. We were not going to back down. We were not going to go out without a fight. We were homemade warriors. The minute we heard the kitchen window break, we jumped into action.

As we stepped foot in the kitchen, we saw the intruder on the floor. We looked down at him in shock. I, for one, was thinking to myself: what is going on here? This was not one of our murderers; it was my new neighbor, Reggie.

Tania never met Reggie, so she was still ready to hit him with the coffee pot. I quickly stopped her. She looked at me, confused.

"Why are you stopping me?" Tania asked. "We need to get this guy!"

"I agree, but this is not the guy. This is my new neighbor," I said.

"What?" Tania shouted.

"Please, don't hurt me, it seems I've hurt myself enough," Reggie pleaded.

Tania put down the coffee pot. I helped Reggie up. Thankfully, he did not seem too hurt after crashing through my kitchen window. We helped him to the TV room and put him on the sofa. He seemed okay, thankfully, but now he was going to have to explain himself.

"What are you doing jumping through my kitchen window?" I asked.

"I'm sorry, Dimples. I saw a woman looking through your kitchen window and going around the back of your house. I thought you might be in trouble, so I sprang into action," he explained.

"That's my kind of guy," Tania said. "You can be my neighbor any day. Wait, did he just call you Dimples?"

"What are you saying? Are you saying it is okay for him to jump through my kitchen window?" I retorted. "And yes, he called me Dimples. It's his special name for me."

"Well, in my defense, I was trying to help. It's not like I was trying in any way to hurt you or hit you with my car or anything like that," Reggie noted.

"That was a mistake. This is different," I said.

"You're right, I was trying to protect you and you were trying to kill me," Reggie suggested.

"What is he talking about?" Tania asked. "You hit him with your car? Why does he have a special name for you, exactly?"

I explained what happened yesterday morning, when I accidentally tapped his moving van while he was moving in next door. Everyone makes mistakes. I guess it was sweet that he would jump through glass for me after our first meeting. I had to be more open-minded about this. He was in the right and I overreacted. So I decided to do the best thing possible, in my view: forget everything that happened entirely and quickly move on to a new topic.

"Great day we're having today, right?" I pointed out. Tania and Reggie stared back at me in disbelief. "I hear we are going to have record-high temperatures today."

"Let me introduce myself; I'm Sheila's friend Tania. I am not a robber. I rang the front doorbell, but she didn't answer, so I went around back," Tania explained.

"That makes perfect sense now," Reggie said. "Sheila is lucky to have a friend like you."

How sweet that the two of them were bonding. But let's get back to business.

"You know you will be paying to fix my kitchen window, right?" I

33

stated.

"Of course, send me the bill. Again, I'm very sorry," he volunteered.

"What do you do for a living?" Tania asked Reggie. She was desperate to change the subject. She wanted to know about my new neighbor.

"I'm a theater reporter," Reggie said.

"That's crazy! Sheila was a crime reporter, and now she has her own online publishing company. I'm her best friend and copy editor. We went to college together," Tania said.

Again, the two of them were getting all cozy. First, my best friend just lets herself in my back door, and then my new neighbor jumps in my kitchen window. My life is so weird. This stuff only happens to me.

If I stop to reflect a bit, it is nice to have two people that care for me, though. Well, I'm not sure how much Reggie cares about me, but I must admit, I am a bit interested in him. Tania is the best friend a person could ask for. She's honest, blunt, and caring. She's also adventurous.

Soon after we met in college, I was dating a stereotypical fraternity boy. I was stupid, but he was cute and popular, so I was intrigued. At a party, he slipped something in my drink. Tania saw him. She slapped that drink out of my hand and she slapped him next. I was stunned. I didn't know what happened. Once she explained, I slapped him too, and Tania and I left the party together. We laugh about it now, but what if I'd had that drink? What could have happened to me? She saved me that night from God knows what. I am lucky to have her as my friend.

She went into the bathroom and came back with a pack of toilet paper. She was ready for action. She convinced me to go back to the fraternity house and decorate the outside with toilet paper. It wasn't something I would think of or normally do, but it just made sense to Tania.

I was shy and timid at first, but I went along. Why not? Nobody saw us. We didn't get caught, and it was liberating; it was freeing. I was taking back the power he tried to take away from me. I wasn't going to be a victim.

After we finished with the fraternity house, we went back to our dorm room and talked all night. We'd do that a lot, even up to today. Tania is a great sounding board. She listens. Her views and actions might be a little bit unorthodox, but that is okay with me. In fact, that is just great with me.

"I bet you guys have never had such an off-the-wall morning," Reggie said.

Tania and I looked at each other. "Not really. And we've done a lot of crazy things together through the years," Tania said. "But Sheila's morning yesterday was even worse."

"I guess hitting your neighbor while he's moving in is pretty weird," Reggie laughed.

"That's not what I mean, Reggie. After she hit you, she went to her usual morning breakfast spot, and she witnessed a murder. Two cops killed a Black man, and she saw it all," Tania reported.

Reggie's eyes widened. He was alarmed and stunned and just shocked. His skin looked caramel, but he was still Black. He felt that man's pain instantly. Then, he stiffened up. He became very serious. He became very focused.

"I think our country is at a crossroads," he started. "I wonder which way we'll go. Will we continue to do nothing, or will we rise to the occasion? I hope we don't ignore what's going on. I hope we don't just say it's an isolated incident."

Tania and I stared at him. We were quiet. We were listening intently to his every word. He was teaching us right now. We were his students, and we were learning.

"It shouldn't be a choice of do we want law and order or do we want social justice," he continued. "Why can't we want both? Why can't we *get* both? Don't we deserve both? We should empower good police officers and expect that they will protect us. But at the same time, we should recognize the systemic racism that still exists in our country and fight to end it. It is not right for police officers to target and even kill African Americans like me. And when we say that, we are not standing up against police, we are standing up for justice and the American way. That's what we all deserve, right?"

I was stunned. I couldn't talk. I wasn't prepared to have such a deep conversation so early in the morning. My brain cells were still just waking up. I looked at Tania and she was quiet too, but that didn't last for long.

"I agree," Tania said. "We should get everything. We should get good policing *and* an end to racism. I think we divide into camps too often and turn common sense into wedge issues. Some things are, or at least should be, universal."

"So what are we going to do about it?" Reggie asked.

Again, Tania and I were silent and stared at each other quietly for a while.

"We should stand up!" Tania said. She literally stood up.

"I agree!" Reggie said. Reggie literally stood up too.

I sat there a bit, amazed. I was the only one still seated at this point, while the two of them were ready to start a revolution or something. What should I do? Should I stand up too? Witnessing the murder made me angry. I witnessed a clear injustice. I can't imagine how Reggie felt as a Black man, but it must be even worse than I was feeling. When I was in the police station, I was ready to act. I was going to solve the murder. Now I felt stronger than ever that was the right instinct. I witnessed an atrocity, and I had to do something about it. I had to solve this murder. There was no other choice, and now I had the right team to help me.

"Are you with us?" Tania asked. She looked down at me.

"Of course I am," I said as I, too, rose to my feet.

"Great, so what's our first move?" Reggie asked.

That was it. That was the moment I realized Reggie was sincere and forthright, but he was the kind of guy that needed to be guided. In that moment, a lightbulb went off in my head. Reggie was a theater reporter. I was sure he'd seen a lot of plays. I was sure he appreciated high drama. Of course he did. That speech was a great monologue. I was transfixed by his little speech. It moved me, for sure, but we had to do much more.

We had to develop a plan. We had to decide what to do next. That plan might not be so dramatic or inspired, but that didn't make it any less important. I was going to have to take charge and, you know what? That was just fine with me.

"I agree. We have to do something," I said with great authority. "We have to have a plan."

"Maybe we should go back to the scene," suggested Reggie.

"Maybe we should take our issues straight to the governor or the mayor," Tania added.

"Those are good ideas, but the police have probably combed the scene, and the governor is in the middle of reelection, so he is not going to help us. I could talk to Leslie about the mayor, but we all know how flighty our mayor is, right?" I noted.

"So what do we do?" Reggie interrupted. "We can't do nothing."

"Of course we won't do nothing!" I snapped back. "Yesterday I gave my statement to Lieutenant Crooks. That's where we start, with him."

"Crooks is a jerk," Tania responded.

"I know, but I have to see what the officials are doing with this case. And I enlisted a friend at the police station too, because we know Crooks isn't going to do the right thing unless it hits him upside the head," I noted.

"You know these people?" Reggie asked.

"I told you, she was a crime reporter," Tania said.

In that moment, they both started walking toward the front door. They were ready to go on the next stage of this journey. They clearly agreed with my course of action, which worked for me, but there was a slight problem.

"Let's go, Dimples," Reggie said.

"Let's get a move on, Sheila," Tania added.

They both looked back disapprovingly at me because I did not follow them to the front door. I looked down to draw attention to the fact that they were both dressed, and I was still in my pajamas and housecoat. I couldn't go anywhere looking like this. They caught on, so I marched up to my room to quickly change. I wasn't the type to waste time or take forever to get ready. I did what I had to do upstairs and returned back downstairs, dressed and ready to go.

In that moment, we marched out the front door together, all three of us, to go to the police station and solve this murder.

CHAPTER 9
THINGS TURN UPSIDE DOWN

Me and my crew entered the police station with one goal in mind: getting to the bottom of this murder. We were going to first see what the police were doing, then we were ready to step in, assuming the police were unwilling to police two of their own. I hoped the police were doing the right thing, personally; I didn't want to be a self-made police officer. However, I wanted to see justice. What those police did to that man was wrong, period.

So I stepped up to the counter and demanded to speak with Lieutenant Crooks. I gave him my statement yesterday, so he was the guy to talk to. Of course, I was ready to go to my Plan B person, but before I enlisted the help of Anthony again, I had to hear from Crooks first. Maybe he was doing the right thing and solving this case. Who am I kidding? I know Crooks is stumbling through, just hoping to get this case closed as quickly as possible.

The clerk made us wait as he went to fetch Crooks. Was he really looking for Crooks? Was he really going to let us talk to him? I was not convinced. I don't like to cast bets, but if I did, I would bet the police were about to dismiss us. I was ready to be told I needed to go home and leave this to the police.

"You seem to know your way around here, Dimples," said Reggie.

"Like Tania told you, I was a crime reporter," I stated.

"And she was a good one too," noted Tania.

"I guess so, that clerk knew who you were straight away," Reggie said. "I thought they would have told us to go home by now."

"Me too, which means they're afraid of us," I pointed out. "It shouldn't be taking this long for them to fetch Lieutenant Crooks. It's simple: either we get to talk to him, or they tell us we have to come back later. My guess is they're planning what to say to us right about now. Their response is going to be telling."

In that moment, my mind wandered. If they did let us talk to Crooks, what would I say to him? Would I be confrontational? Would I be deferential? I thought the best approach was to listen first. I was not reporting on a story here. I was a part of this story. I was actually a pretty big part of this story. I was an eyewitness. That sounded crazy as I thought about it. However, it is freeing to face the truth, I think. Knowing the truth and confronting the truth is important. We all need to do it at one point or another, but how we do it is very telling. We can't be dismissive of truth. We have to embrace it in all its messiness.

Yes, sometimes the truth is messy. Sometimes it is inconvenient. But that doesn't mean we have the liberty to just ignore it. We can't look away when things get messy.

"Here he comes," Reggie said, pointing to the clerk as he came back to address us. The clerk said Crooks wanted to speak with us. I looked at Reggie and Tania and the shock was easily seen across all of our faces. This was big. We were not being dismissed. They actually wanted to talk to us.

As we walked through the sea of police officers, they all seemed to be looking at us. It was as if we were dignitaries of some kind. Everyone had to get a glimpse of us. Up ahead I saw Lieutenant Crooks waiting for us at his desk. He seemed happy to see us. He was smiling.

"So good to see you, Sheila," Crooks said. He motioned all of us to sit down. "Who's your crew?"

"This is Reggie, and this is Tania," I said.

"So great to meet you both," Crooks said.

Now I knew something was wrong. Crooks was never happy to see me, and he would never invite civilians in to just chat like this. He had something he wanted to tell us. He was eager to speak his mind about this case, and he wanted us to hear what he had to say.

Tania also looked stoic, as if she was bracing for the worst. Reggie seemed attentive. I think he wanted to hear Crooks out.

"Like I said, it is just wonderful to see you, though I have to admit you must be psychic or something, Sheila, because I was going to call you today," Crooks noted. "I was going to pick up my phone and give you a call for sure."

"In that case, I guess it's good we decided to stop by," I responded. "We saved you the call. I hope you understand we are not here to harass you. We want to see justice done."

"Of course you do, Sheila. That's what we all want. We're all on the same page here. We're all friends here—"

"Yes, well, we're not going to let you cops roll us," Tania interrupted. "This is going to get done right. We're not going to sit back as you all try to protect your own."

That was Tania for you, blunt as ever. She was dead on. We weren't going to let the police cover this up. You would think Tania's remarks would have upset a police officer like Crooks, but he did not flinch. He was not upset at all. He was still practically exuberant.

"That would never be our approach, dear lady," Crooks said politely. "We are here to serve the public, not assault them. We are here to protect, not do anything that would harm or divide the people of our little town. We live in a tight neighborhood here. I assure you, we have the public's best interests at heart."

"So what do you have to tell us?" I asked.

"What do you mean?" Crooks replied.

"You wouldn't have let us back here if you didn't want to say something to us. I was expecting to be ignored or dismissed, but instead I am sitting here at your desk. I've never been treated so kindly. So what's the angle?"

"My dear Sheila, always with the questions. You can't help yourself," Crooks responded. "But you are right. I have news. We solved the case, actually. Well, we haven't found the guilty parties, but we have come to some solid conclusions. The dead man's name is Arthur Jones, or was Arthur Jones. We know because his wife, Shanice, reported him missing. She identified the body earlier this morning. It was actually a lucky break, because all of Mr. Jones's things were missing. You told us he had a cell phone, but there wasn't a cell phone at the scene; he also didn't have a wallet. So it was good his wife called us concerned about his whereabouts. We've concluded this was a mugging gone wrong."

"Are you serious?" Tania yelled.

"That can't be," Reggie said. "Dimples said she saw two police officers killing him."

"Who is Dimples, exactly?" Crooks asked.

"Don't change the topic, Crooks; that's just what he calls me," I said.

Crooks laughed, but quickly caught himself. "It's funny you bring that up about the police officers because we looked into that part of Sheila's story," Crooks said. "Sheila was unable to identify the female killer aside from her hair color and jewelry, so we focused on the male. We looked at every police officer and nobody matched our dear Sheila's description. Also, all the police cars were accounted for that morning. As a result, we concluded that these were two very desperate people looking to get some cash and must have been dressed as police officers."

"That's ridiculous!" I yelled. I stood up for everyone to hear me. "I know what I saw! I saw a police car parked across the street! Those two people were police officers!"

"Please be calm, Sheila," Crooks said.

"Don't tell her to be calm!" Tania shouted.

"Yeah, don't tell Dimples to be calm," Reggie added.

I guess we were making a scene because someone obviously called DA Clarence from his office to come over to us. He appeared holding a box filled with papers, as if he was maybe moving his desk. As he got closer to us, he tripped and fell on the floor. I bent down to help him gather everything that fell out of the box and put it back. He was grateful for the help.

"Are you leaving before the election results even come in? You're not governor yet, you know," I laughed.

"No, these are actually my father's things. He passed away last week, and I stumbled upon some of his things. These were his personal letters. Some of them sweet love letters, actually. I've been going through them here at work. I was ready to load them back into my car when I was told to come here to address your shouting," Clarence said.

"I'm sorry to hear about your father," I noted. "I don't want to make your life any harder right now, but you have an issue within this police department."

"Lieutenant Crooks says otherwise. The man you found dead was the victim of a robbery," Clarence said. "By the way, you were always very astute. What do you think of this suit I'm wearing?"

"That can't be true," I asserted forcefully. "And your suit is very nice."

"Thanks, appearances matter, you know. But back to this case. What other conclusion is there? You say the victim had a cell phone and he was receiving calls, but there was no cell phone found at the scene. The man also had no wallet. Crooks immediately concluded it was a robbery, but I told him we had to identify the body and see if we had an officer matching your description before we came to any conclusions. We can't have any shadows falling over our good police. We have to follow every lead. Lieutenant Crooks says there are no officers matching your description and all the police cars were elsewhere at the time. Furthermore, the widow came forward this morning and positively identified Arthur Jones. What else can we do?"

"Obviously nothing," I replied.

"What?" Tania asked, astonished.

"That's it?" Crooks added.

"It seems like you've all done your job," I said. "When you find the killers, please let me know. I don't think I'll be able to put this behind me until this case is closed and the killers are found and prosecuted. One more tiny question, you are still looking for these muggers, right?"

"Of course we are," Crooks responded.

I walked off. Tania and Reggie followed me.

"So that's it?" Reggie asked.

"Nope," I responded. "I've got another idea in mind. We're not through here yet."

I saw Anthony down the hall, and he saw me. He quickly but quietly waved me over. He had something for me.

"I've been looking into what you said yesterday," Anthony reported. "The wife did positively identify her husband as the dead man. We are checking everything out against our records, but I saw her come in this morning and she was very upset. She seemed sincere to me. I wrote down all her information for you."

He passed me a piece of paper and a photo album.

"Come into this office," he said. All four of us went into a private office. "I put together this little photo album for you to look at. These are pictures of every male police officer that is active and those that have retired within the last five years. I want you to have a look. If we do have bad police officers, I want to know. Maybe you can identify the male you saw here."

Anthony was tried and true. I knew he would help me. I carefully looked at every picture in the album. I thought to myself, I don't want to miss anything. I want to be precise. I was looking and looking for what seemed like forever, and I now had a conclusion I had to share.

"Crooks was right," I said.

"What do you mean, Crooks was right?" Tania asked, confused.

"The man I saw kill this Arthur Jones is not here. I am sure of it. I guess they were people dressed like police, as Crooks said. But this was no robbery. This was a murder for sure. But if they aren't police, who are they? And why would they want to kill Arthur Jones?"

CHAPTER 10
DEVISING THE BEST WAY FORWARD

How could I have been so wrong? Was I too sure of myself? Was I too guided by what I saw with my eyes to really see what was going on? What was going on? A man was killed, that's what was going on. I had to focus on the job in front of me and think about everything I know.

In fact, I think we were all thinking. Tania, Reggie, and I decided to take one car to the police station. Now we were all in that car again, going back to my house. Reggie was our designated driver. I was too distracted to drive, and Tania was too emotional. She couldn't believe the police were not behind it. The silence was palpable. I think we were all just processing what had happened.

"So I guess it's over, Dimples?" Reggie asked, finally breaking the silence.

"Are you kidding?" Tania said. "They still have not found those two murderers. All they have is a theory of the case."

"It all seems to add up though," he said. "Even Dimples backs Lieutenant Crooks up now."

"Not really, she just acknowledges the guy that killed Arthur was not in the photo album. What if there are other cops Anthony didn't get pictures of?"

"No, let's not blame Anthony," I said. "We have to think about this objectively. The man wasn't in those photos, and I don't think Anthony would leave anyone out of the pictures on purpose."

"But maybe it was an accident," Tania said.

"Maybe, but I don't think it helps us right now to second-guess Anthony. We have to move forward, not backward," I said.

"So how do we do that?" asked Reggie.

My mind was racing. I was flashing back to the alley, thinking about what I saw. I saw them killing him, so I ran into Harry's for help. Harry got his bat, and he was ready for a fight. Soon all my friends were there, helping me through. I was surrounded by my people. It was freeing, having my own backup squad.

Arthur Jones was not as lucky. He did not have anyone to support him. He did not have anyone to save him. He was all alone in the alley. Those killers took his life, and there was little he could do in his own defense. He struggled. He screamed. He tried to fight back. None of it worked out for him.

It was in that moment, it came to me. He wasn't alone really, he was just alone in the alley. He had his own support system. Arthur was turning to people, and so should we. The answer on how to move forward with this investigation, of sorts, was in my hands all along. Sometimes it's the easy things that take so long to figure out. Over-thinking this wasn't the answer; following the facts was what was going to see us through.

"I have it!" I yelled. "Stop the car! We have to turn around!"

Reggie slammed on the brakes. The car came to a screeching halt. Tania and I flew forward before flying back in our seats. I could hear the brakes and smell the rubber on the road as the tires ground to a stop. We were in the middle of the road and now we were just stopped. There was a car behind us, but luckily the driver of that car was able to slam on his brakes to avoid hitting us from behind.

"What are you doing?" I asked Reggie.

"You said to stop, Dimples," he replied.

"I did not mean literally," I said.

The man in the car behind us was mad. He was fuming. He got out of his car and marched up to Reggie's window.

"What the hell are you doing?" the man yelled.

The window was down, and Reggie was in a panic. He turned to me. "What do I do? What do I say?"

"I don't know," I said. "Make something up."

Of course, Tania sprang into action and did the unexpected. I should have known. She was curling her hair with her fingers. Every time she curls her hair with her fingers, she's thinking about a crazy plan of action.

There was a blanket in the back seat of the car where she was sitting. She quickly grabbed the blanket, folded it in a ball, and shoved it under her shirt. From there she started panting wildly. I had no idea what she was doing, but Reggie was totally in sync with her plan. He rolled down the window to address the angry man.

"What the hell are you doing?" the man yelled again.

"I am so sorry," Reggie responded.

"Not half as sorry as you're going to be!" the man screamed.

"Shut up, you ass!" Tania yelled. "Get over yourself! We are dealing with a real situation here!"

"You're going to be dealing with me in a second, missy," the man said.

"Please excuse me and my wife. We are expecting and her water just broke. We have to get to the hospital!" Reggie said. I was about to talk when Reggie covered my mouth with his hand. "She's our midwife. She can't speak English. Don't listen to her."

He was silencing me; Reggie was keeping me quiet. How dare he! So I did what any self-respecting woman would do in this situation: I bit down on his hand. He screamed and removed his hand from my mouth quickly.

"The man is mistaken," I said.

"No, I am not. She does speak some English, but not much. Are you okay, sir?" Reggie said.

"Yes, I'll be okay. My apologies. Don't let me stop you. I won't get in your way," the man noted.

After that, Reggie rolled up the window and we drove off. "What was that all about?" I asked.

"What do you mean, Dimples?" Reggie asked. "Again, you said we should stop, so I stopped."

"The answer about what our next step should be was always in my hand. Arthur did have support. He called his wife. I heard them on the phone together. Furthermore, Anthony gave me her name and address. We should start by talking to her," I said.

"That's it?" Reggie asked.

"What do you mean that's it?" I asked.

"Couldn't you have just said that without yelling stop?"

"Maybe I could have, but it just hit me in the moment."

"Yeah, and we almost got hit in the moment too."

"Stop complaining and turn around so we can go talk to his widow."

"Are you sure you two just met yesterday? You sound like an old married couple to me," Tania interrupted.

I could have sworn I saw Reggie smile after Tania's remark. Maybe I was just imagining it.

Anyway, we were at Arthur's house soon enough, and parked in the driveway were two cars: a silver Camry and a black BMW. This was going to be a family with varying tastes and stations in life for sure. The house was modest. The neighborhood was decent. It was outside of Harmony, which is why I didn't know who Arthur was. Everything seemed normal enough, I guess.

We walked up to the front door and rang the doorbell. We were greeted by Shanice, Arthur's widow. I could tell it was her because she had obviously been crying, as you would expect from a widow.

"Today is just not a good day. I really am not interested in what you're selling," Shanice said.

She was going through a horrible time, so I wasn't going to drag this out. "I saw your husband killed in the alley yesterday, and I was wondering if we could talk."

"What do you mean?" Shanice asked.

"I saw him killed in that alley. I ran for help, but it was too late. I gave my statement to the police yesterday and we just came from the station. I think they have this murder all wrong, and I think you can help us solve it."

She was obviously shocked by what I said, which I'm sure is why she let us in to talk. The house was nice. It was tidy and well-organized. There were a lot of pictures on the walls, but they were just of Arthur and Shanice, so I guessed they didn't have any children.

As we walked into the sitting room, Shanice introduced us to an older woman sitting there on the sofa. The woman was stately and well-dressed. Her hair had a distinctive gray patch that shaped the right side of her face.

"This is Yolanda, Arthur's mother," Shanice said.

"Who are these people, Shanice?" Yolanda asked.

"This woman says she saw Arthur murdered," Shanice answered.

At that statement, Yolanda kept quiet. She was unmoved. She didn't even get up from the sofa to talk to us. This was not the reaction I would have expected from a mother that just lost her son.

"Two people disguised as police officers killed him. I saw it all. It was horrific. The police think it was a mugging, but it wasn't. He was in Harry's Deli and someone called him on the phone. Whatever they said caused him to leave Harry's in a hurry. They lured him out of Harry's with the intent to kill him in that alley. I know it."

"You must be mistaken," Yolanda interrupted. "Arthur was far too smart to be lured anywhere."

"Yolanda is right, I'm afraid," Shanice added. "Arthur was very smart."

"Is that BMW out there his?" Reggie asked.

"No, it's mine," Yolanda said.

"Actually, we just bought a used BMW last week and Arthur was very proud of it," Shanice said.

"That's it; maybe the call was about his car. Maybe someone was calling him about his car, so he ran out to see what was going on," I theorized.

"Who would do that?" Yolanda asked.

"Somebody he knew. Somebody that knew how proud he was of the car and wanted him dead," I answered.

"My, my, this one does have a vivid imagination," Yolanda laughed. She excused herself at that point and said she had an errand to run. Now it was just Shanice and us in the house.

"Did Arthur have any enemies?" I asked.

"No, none at all," Shanice answered. "He was about to get himself a new job or something. He decided to make a career change very suddenly. His best friend, Tom, was upset. He was hounding us to know why Arthur decided to go it alone. I was shocked myself. But Arthur insisted he was about to come into a bunch of money. I was skeptical. Arthur was a very savvy guy. He had good instincts. He always had a plan."

"Can you give us Tom's information?" I asked.

"Of course," Shanice said politely. She wrote his name, home address, work address, and some phone numbers on a piece of paper and handed it to me.

"Thank you so much. I'm so sorry for your loss," I said. "One more tiny question; were Arthur and Yolanda close?"

Shanice shook her head no. We thanked her, and Reggie, Tania, and I left for the car.

"Well, that was a dead end," Reggie noted.

"I'm not sure I would agree," I said.

Meeting Shanice was the right move. This was the logical next step and we followed it through. She seemed like a grieving widow that was getting over the loss of her husband, even though it seemed from their call the marriage wasn't working. I can't understand how that feels exactly, since I was never married, but when my father walked out on us, I was hurting at first. I felt that loss very deeply at the time. It was a loss that shaped who I am today, as a matter of fact. But dealing with loss can be freeing. Moving on is the best remedy, in my opinion.

"What are you thinking, Sheila?" Tania asked.

"I think we learned a lot here. Shanice is certainly grieving. I think she misses Arthur a lot, but what was curious to me was how cold Yolanda seemed. She was not the vision of what I would picture a grieving mother to be. And we also learned about this Tom person. My friends, I believe we have our first two suspects. We have to consider that maybe the two killers were hired by someone that lured Arthur into that alley so his or her two lackies could murder Arthur. I think we're looking at a murder-for-hire plot."

CHAPTER 11
FOLLOWING THE MONEY

Everyone has to work. We all need to earn a living and pay our bills. Fortunately, I work from home, but I still work. Owning your own online publishing company can be crazy and stressful. When I started this venture, I was very scared. I thought to myself, will it work? Will readers respond well to it? Will I be able to make a living? The journey was well worth it. I'm my own boss and I love it.

However, I couldn't have done it without Tania. You need a cheerleader sometimes, cheering you on to ensure your success. Tania has always been my cheerleader, but I won't tell her that. She hates cheerleaders. We both do, actually. We had a bad time with cheerleaders at college and we never really recovered.

When I was thinking about starting my own publishing company, I felt like I could do it so much better than Duke. It was a rebellion, of sorts. I needed to make my own way in the world. So, of course, I ran the idea by Tania first. She saw it was something I wanted to do right away, so she was quick to encourage me. Tania saw that twinkle in my eye, which she says I have when I get an idea. Honestly, I don't think she sees anything for real, but she says she does because she knows it energizes me when she perks up and gets all excited about something.

I am happy asking the questions, but settling on an answer is sometimes elusive to me. I was afraid to go out on my own, and Tania knew it. So what did she do? She volunteered to join me as my copy editor. So she comes to my house each day and we write, edit, and publish everything together. We are not millionaires, but it is working, and people are responding to our work.

After our visit to Shanice's house, we returned to my house and started working away. Finding Arthur's murderers doesn't pay the bills. Besides, Reggie had more unpacking to do, so he went back home and said he would meet us in a few hours so we could visit Arthur's friend Tom. The idea was that Tania and I would get some work done while he straightened out his new house, but of course, we couldn't stop thinking about Arthur.

"What did you mean when you said we have two suspects?" Tania asked.

"As I see it, we have two people worth looking at for murdering Arthur," I said.

"That's not possible," Tania responded.

"Why?" I asked.

"Because we haven't met anyone that remotely matches the description of the two killers you saw in the alley just yet, so how can we have suspects?"

"Here's how I figure it, Tania: we are either going to look at the people around Arthur and the killers are going to turn up, or the killers were hired to kill Arthur by someone he knows. We could very well be looking at a murder-for-hire situation here, as I said earlier, if you were listening."

"And you think Yolanda or Tom would hire someone to kill Arthur?"

"I think it's worth the effort to look into, and if they didn't, maybe they will lead us to our killers."

"Yolanda is Arthur's mother. How could a mother kill her child?" Tania said.

"I don't know, but I do know Yolanda was very cold and detached, and she just heard her son was murdered. That's not normal behavior. Shanice was obviously crying, but not Yolanda."

"I see what you mean. It was rather odd behavior, but everyone deals with grief in their own way, Sheila. I'm not convinced a mother would do this, or in this case, hire someone else to do this."

"We have to follow the leads where they take us and hope more come as a result. A good story is all about sourcing. We have to compile and interview all our sources, and hopefully, in the end, we'll get the true story."

"Speaking of stories, what's up with Reggie?" Tania asked.

"What do you mean?"

"He's calling you Dimples and you're not saying a word. In fact, when he calls you that, you blush a bit. It's very cute, and so is he."

"It's nothing," I responded coyly. "I'm just being neighborly."

That second, the front doorbell rang and, not surprisingly, it was Reggie. He had changed his clothes. He was in a navy-blue, three-piece suit, and you could tell by looking at him he thought he looked good. His hair was nicely slicked back and his crisp, white shirt showed off his white teeth and his charming grin.

"Come on in," I said.

"Don't mind if I do," Reggie replied confidently. He strolled into the house as if he owned the place.

"Where are you going?" Tania asked.

"When in the presence of two beautiful ladies, one must dress to impress," he said. Tania and I smiled. It was sweet of him to dress up for us. Gosh, how long had it been since a man dressed up for me? Well, a long time.

"I think we should talk to Tom to see what he's up to and why he was harassing Arthur about his life decisions, don't you ladies agree?" Reggie said.

"I agree with Reggie. We have a plan, and I think we should see it through. We have to pay Tom a visit, for sure," Tania said.

We all filed back into the car and I sat on something hard and yelped. I jumped up right away. What did I sit on? I looked down and it was a cell phone.

"Sorry about that. I'm always leaving my cell phone places," Reggie explained.

No big deal. I gave him his phone and the three of us were off on our latest adventure to find these killers. We were a new team, but we complemented each other so well. Reggie had the presence, Tania had the go-getter spirit, and I had the skills to ask the right questions and get the right answers.

We circled and circled Tom's office building, but we could not find a parking space. So we double-parked and left Tania with the car. As Reggie and I entered the office, there was a lot of commotion. Tom's secretary was irate. She was on the phone yelling at what seemed to be a close friend or family member.

"I can't take this! His clients are so rude! They treat me like trash! I'm a person! I have feelings! If Tom says he is busy, I can't just let people in his office. I have to respect my boss. I have to do my job. I can't just let anyone in there," his secretary said.

"I don't mean to disturb you, but we need to talk to Tom," I said.

"Do you have an appointment?" she asked.

"No, but we have urgent business to discuss," Reggie said.

"Of course, everyone has urgent business. He is in with someone right now," the secretary reported. However, we were in luck because the door to his office swung open. Tom was showing out his guest, and to our surprise, it was Yolanda. I could not believe it. If this guy was harassing her son, why would she be visiting him?

"So we meet again," Yolanda said. "If I didn't know better, I would think you were following me."

"I was thinking the same about you," I retorted.

"What is it you do for a living again?" Yolanda asked.

"I'm a journalist," I said.

"Figures," Yolanda noted. She gave me a fake smile and left the office after collecting her jacket and purse.

At that point, Reggie declared that we knew Tom's friend Arthur and we needed to discuss his relationship with him. Tom looked stunned, as if he was being accused of something.

"Are you sure you two aren't police officers?" Tom said as he laughed.

"No, we're actually both journalists," I noted. At that point, he showed us into his office politely, but it was clear he did not want us there.

"So you're going to see these two without an appointment too?" the secretary asked.

"Don't bother yourself, these two are fine," Tom said. This response angered his secretary, and she was ready to blow up. She stood up from her desk and her anger was easy to see.

"I can't work like this! People can't just be coming and going whenever. Furthermore, Yolanda always comes here without an appointment and just lets herself in. She doesn't even acknowledge my presence. It's disrespectful. You're disrespectful! I quit!" With that, the secretary marched out of the office.

"I'm sorry. She's a bit of a control freak. I was going to fire her this afternoon anyway. I've already sent the 'Help Wanted' notice to the newspaper to start running tomorrow, as a matter of fact," Tom explained.

His office was very minimalist, but very tidy and well put together. He was an organized man that didn't like mess, which is probably why his secretary did not rub him the right way. Her volatility seemed to be the exact opposite of his personality.

"I witnessed Arthur's murder," I explained.

"That must have been horrible for you," Tom said. "I'm sorry you had to go through that."

"She's a tough lady," Reggie said.

"I'm sure she is," Tom replied. "Why are you here to see me? I did not know Arthur well, I'm afraid."

"You seem to know his mother well," I said.

"Yes, we've been partners for a long time. She introduced me to her son. I was about to partner with him too, but he pulled out," Tom noted.

"Wait just one second," Reggie said. "I want to write this down. I don't want to forget anything you say." He emptied his pockets on Tom's desk until he pulled out a small notepad and a pen.

"There's not much to write, I'm afraid. I buy and sell real estate. Some of it I hold and manage and other properties I sell. I was about to buy my first property with Arthur. We picked out a great property and he pulled out. He said he found another way to make good money. He blew me off and I was left in the breeze. I was understandably upset, right?"

"Makes sense," Reggie said.

"Where were you the morning Arthur was killed?" I interrupted with my very pointed question.

"I was here doing work. I got here early, and you are welcome to ask my secretary, well, my former secretary," Tom responded.

"Do you know of anyone with two different-colored eyes? One would be grayish and cloudy?" I asked.

"No, I would remember that if I did," Tom answered calmly.

"One more tiny question. What about a woman with platinum hair and pink tips?" I asked.

"Nobody like that comes to mind either," Tom answered. "Are we done with this now?"

Our interview was clearly over. Reggie wrote down the info on Tom's former secretary and tried to gather his things from Tom's desk before we went back to the car, where Tania was eager to hear what we learned. I reported it was a dead end, but we did run into Yolanda. In that second, I looked over at Reggie to see if he had anything he wanted to share. He looked embarrassed.

"Is everything okay?" I asked him.

"I forgot my cell phone in Tom's office, Dimples. I have to go back and get it," Reggie said.

Tania laughed as he ran out the door and back into Tom's office. Tania looked back at me and said, "He's a very nice man, and he's really cute, don't you think?"

"I guess," I said quickly.

"You dodged my questions earlier, but I can see that sparkle in your eye," Tania said. I shushed her with my hand. I did not want to talk about Reggie. Romance was the last thing on my mind. I had to stay focused on what we were doing here. Once Reggie returned, we would have to discuss our next move. Arthur Jones's murder was going to be solved. I was determined to get to the bottom of this whole sordid affair, if Reggie ever got out of that office and back in this car. It seemed like we were waiting a long time for Reggie to return to the car, but we waited patiently, nonetheless.

When Reggie got back, he was eager to talk. He was practically bursting at the seams to tell us something.

"Guess what?" he said. "I went back in the office and Tom's door was cracked open a bit. Before I went in, I heard Yolanda's voice. She must have been waiting somewhere for us to leave before she went back in the office with Tom. So I waited for her to leave before I told Tom I returned for my cell phone. I guess leaving it everywhere helped out because as I went back to retrieve it, I overheard Yolanda telling Tom he should avoid us at all costs because she did not want us poking around in their business together."

I knew she was suspicious for sure now. Yolanda had something going on we still did not fully understand, at least not yet. And I bet, once we found out more about her business dealings, it would point us to Arthur's killers. I was sure of it.

CHAPTER 12
OUR NEXT MOVE COMES INTO FOCUS

Every week, we would have a block party on our cul-de-sac. Well, not a traditional block party, more like a dinner party, I guess. We would gather for dinner as a group. Every week, we would alternate houses so everyone got a chance to host. Our cul-de-sac had six houses, including mine, and six very different families lived in each house. We were a melting pot for sure.

I always got the sense Majesta didn't like these events because I had to leave her for a long stretch alone in the house. When I was changing into my clothes for the dinner, she stared up at me as if to say, "You aren't going to leave me alone here, right?"

I responded, "It's okay. I'll be back soon."

Regardless of Majesta's disapproving eye, I had to go this week. This week was special because it was Reggie's first dinner. He wanted to come to my house first so we could walk over together. I guess he was a bit shy. The doorbell rang and I opened it to see Reggie there with a dozen roses.

"That's so sweet, but I hate flowers," I said.

"I will remember that, but they are not for you, Dimples. They are for Ebony," Reggie said.

Of course they were. How stupid of me to assume they were for me. I brushed off the embarrassment and off we went to Sam and Ebony's house. They were a biracial couple with two middle school children, one girl and one boy. Their story was very interesting. Ebony's parents were not happy she was going to marry a white man. It was a low moment in their relationship for sure. But, despite the backlash from her family, Ebony decided to marry Sam regardless.

The wedding was small but elegant. It was a fun affair, despite all the pain that preceded it. Everyone in attendance had a great time. It was a success. Sam's family continued to support the couple and were very active in the raising of their two children, but Ebony's parents seldom came around. Their expectation was that Ebony would call off the wedding and when that didn't happen, they played a much more distant role in Ebony's life.

"It's great to meet you," Ebony said to Reggie. "Welcome to the neighborhood."

"Thank you so much," Reggie said. "Did Sheila tell you how we first met?"

"Yes," Ebony laughed. "Don't feel bad, that's just Sheila. One time she wanted to cut down a tree in her front yard and she was determined to do it herself. I don't know why, but she was. She was distracted by a fire truck passing our little street and the tree ended up in our front yard."

"In that case, I guess I should be flattered," laughed Reggie.

At that moment, Sam came from upstairs, happy to see all of us. "Welcome, Reggie," Sam said. "The kids had some questions about their homework. We settled everything. I hope I gave them correct advice, though."

Sam shook Reggie's hand and we all made our way to the dining room. I knew it was going to be a fun night filled with a lot of great conversation. Reggie and Sam seemed to be getting along famously. Ebony and I left them alone to go to the kitchen.

"So what do you think of him?" Ebony asked with excitement.

"Reggie seems very nice," I responded.

"He is very cute, and he's also a reporter," Ebony noted.

"What are you getting at, exactly?" I responded, knowing what she was getting at. She wanted to set me up.

"You aren't getting any younger, girl," she said.

In that moment, she sounded like my mother and brother. I know everyone wanted to see me with someone because they wanted to see me happy, but I am happy having my independence and hanging out with Majesta. We're a good pair.

"You can't spend all your time with that cat, after all," Ebony said.

"I know, but you know me," I said.

Ebony was fixing a salad as we continued our little chat. I thought volunteering to help would be a good way to change the topic.

"Can I help you with the salad?" I asked.

"It's salad, I'll be fine," Ebony responded. "Now tell me what you really think of Reggie."

She nudged me with her shoulder as if to get some kind of confession out of me, but I had nothing to confess. I liked Reggie a lot and I looked forward to getting to know him. I guess time would tell beyond that. Thankfully, the doorbell rang and I was rescued from the conversation.

We saw Sasha, her husband, Kamal, and his mother, Millie. They were an African American family on our cul-de-sac. Sasha and Kamal were in their fifties, I'd guess. Their children were grown and on their own. Kamal's mother, Millie, was an older woman in her eighties. She had been through a lot in her life. She was a fighter and a survivor. Most recently, she had suffered a stroke, which is what brought her to our little cul-de-sac. Her husband had passed, and Kamal did not want her to be alone, so he insisted she move in with him and Sasha.

The age was visible on Millie's face but she was beautiful, nonetheless. She wore her wrinkles like a badge of honor. She was truly regal. Her hair was short, and her gray was plentiful, but it complemented her plump cheeks and almost girlish curls. I always admired her. I look up to her, I guess. Sometimes our culture teaches us to dismiss our elderly or to treat them as if they were children, but that's just not so. We should learn from other cultures that revere their elderly.

I could see the twinkle in her eye when she first met Reggie. She liked him a lot. She was eager to learn about his background. Reggie engaged with her fully. They shared what seemed like a long conversation. Millie obviously approved of our new neighbor. After she finished talking to Reggie, she marched over to me and said, "Girl, don't let that one get away."

I was embarrassed at first, but Millie was always known for being brutally honest and blunt.

"I don't know what you mean," I said coyly. I knew exactly what she meant, but what else could I say?

"You've been cooped up in that house alone for too long, Sheila. You need a companion, and I'm not talking about that cat. Pets are great, but they are not people," Millie asserted.

In usual Millie style, she just walked off at that point to rejoin the conversation. She wasn't going to stand there waiting for my response. She said what she wanted to say and that was enough for her. Millie wasn't the type to engage in idle chatter. She came to deliver her message to me, and she did, so she could go back to the others having accomplished her goal.

Of course, I was left to deal with her words and consider them. Everyone was so quick to marry me off to the next guy. They were all against me. They didn't understand how much I valued being my own boss.

I am my own person. Once you get married, you become a couple, and I'm not sure I want to be a couple. However, I have to admit, Reggie did pique my interest. I liked having a fellow journalist on the block, and he didn't hold our little car accident against me too much. Also, when I needed help, he sprang into action and has worked hard to help me figure out what truly happened to Arthur Jones.

The doorbell rang again and it was Dawn and Alyssa. They are a young lesbian couple in their twenties. Dawn lived alone in her house here for a year or two before Alyssa moved in. She has been a welcome addition to our street. The two have made a name for themselves as being young but smart. Dawn is a pharmacologist and Alyssa is in law school. They are two very professional women with a great future. Everyone was happy Dawn found someone. I was too, but it put a lot of pressure on me to find someone next.

Dawn was quick to take me to the kitchen. She was excited. She wanted to tell me something. I knew what she was going to say, though. Dawn showed me a huge diamond ring. I saw it coming. Now I was really going to be the last single woman on the block of marrying age. The pressure was going to get even worse for me to finally settle down.

They were probably going to pressure Reggie too. So if we didn't get together, they'd soon switch to getting him to marry someone else. That had to be my plan, to wear them all out to the point that they'd realize I'm a lost cause. They'd have to be convinced Reggie was a better target for their love projections.

"I'm going to propose tonight," Dawn said.

"I'm very happy for you," I responded.

"Alyssa has been a great partner. It's time to make it official," Dawn said.

"I'm sure you will be very happy together," I added.

In the other room, I could see Reggie mingling. He looked over at me and smiled. He walked over to me as if to escape whatever they were discussing.

"They are fixated with marriage, Dimples," Reggie said.

"They mean well," I replied.

"They wanted to know if I have a girlfriend, when I last had a girl-friend, how many girlfriends I've had. It was getting a bit much," Reggie remarked. I understood what he was thinking, having lived here for quite some time. I never guessed men got the same grief as us women over marriage and such. I guess I was wrong. We were in this together now, which made me feel good, I guess. We would be harassed together now.

In the end, all the nagging would be worth it to see Dawn happy. She had a long struggle with disclosing her sexuality. I think she wanted to be lost in the crowd, and being seen with Alyssa made her stand out. She did not like the attention at all, but fortunately, our society has become more accepting. We have a long way to go, but we have also come a long way too. The march towards full gender and sexual preference equality goes on.

Now the house was almost full and the dinner party was in full swing. We were just waiting for our last neighbor. Olivia was always late. She liked making an entrance.

As if on cue, the doorbell rang and there was Olivia in all her glory. Her hair was short, with bangs tracing her face. She had striking, green eyes that stood out all the more because her hair was dyed red, and she wore bright-red lipstick. Olivia had to be in her late fifties or early sixties, but all the plastic surgery masked her true age. I guess, in her profession, you have to keep up appearances. She was a great musical theater stage star. Olivia was known for her Broadway belt, but she was not a classic soprano; in fact, her voice was unusually low for a woman, but, boy, did she know how to use it. Olivia had performed around the world for dignitaries and heads of state.

Tonight, she entered wearing a gold sequin wrap and a one-piece black outfit. Olivia brought her typical bottle of champagne and her commanding sense of self. Once she discovered Reggie was a theater reporter, I'm sure she would be thrilled. Reggie better be ready for her to chat his ear off tonight.

"I am so sorry to be late," Olivia said.

"No worries at all," Ebony responded.

"It looks like everyone is here," Olivia said.

"Yup. Everyone is with us this week."

"Where is our new neighbor?"

Reggie stepped up to answer her call for him. "I'm here. It's so nice to meet you in person," Reggie said. He knew full well who she was, and meeting her in the flesh was a real treat for a theater reporter like him. "I can't tell you how honored I am to meet you."

"Well, now that's an introduction a lady truly loves to hear," Olivia responded. "Are you a theater lover?"

"I am a theater reporter," Reggie answered. "I have written many articles about you, and I've even referenced you in articles I've done of others."

"That's fabulous," Olivia swooned. "I can tell we are going to be fast friends. I am so happy to welcome you to our little block."

Everyone could see Reggie was starstruck, and Olivia was happy to play along. It had been many years since Olivia was on the stage, so I'm sure the attention was welcome. Her star wasn't exactly fading, she was revered, but the days of her getting the starring role had certainly passed. Olivia was having a moment and she was going to soak it up for all it was worth. She adored being adored, so Reggie's interest was very welcome, and something she was going to stoke and not tamp down at all.

Soon, we sat down to eat. Ebony had prepared a feast. The main course was her famous meatloaf. I love meatloaf. Ebony's was the right mix of hearty, salty, and spicy. This meatloaf had just the right kick to it, which was fitting for the conversation. Lots of talk about love and living. As the meatloaf cleared, Dawn rose from her seat to make a proclamation.

"You all know Alyssa has made me so happy. It's been a crazy ride, but the past few years have been amazing for me. I don't want the ride to end, so I have a special request."

Dawn got down on bended knee, pulled out the ring, and gave it to Alyssa. It was a scene out of a fairy tale. Dawn was so excited, and Alyssa looked happy as well.

"Will you do me the honor of being my wife, Alyssa?" Dawn asked.

Alyssa accepted, and the two embraced lovingly. Everyone clapped for the newly engaged couple. It was truly a special occasion!

"As you know, I can't let things go without asking a question. I know you literally just got engaged, but when do you think the wedding will take place?" I asked.

"I can't wait to get married. I think as soon as possible," Dawn said. "And, of course, you are all invited. I want to be surrounded by close friends and family."

"I think we'll have to talk about it. It's all so new," Alyssa added. She looked a bit reserved to me now, but Alyssa was still quite happy for sure.

Now was my opportunity to tell everyone about the murder. We often shared our week with each other, and I wanted feedback. I wanted to see where they thought things stood in my little investigation.

"That boy's family needs your help, Sheila," said Millie. "You have to keep sleuthing."

"We're definitely not going to give up," I said. "The mother is so cold. I think she has to be involved. Just yesterday, we went to his business partner, only to discover he had been partnered with the mother for quite some time as well. Maybe they are in it together."

"I don't know," noted Reggie. "There is something there, but I am not convinced it's murder. I just don't know, but they are certainly hiding something they don't want us to know."

"So you two are doing this together?" Olivia asked, motioning at me and Reggie. Reggie and I looked at each other for a moment and both found ourselves nodding our heads in the affirmative.

"Yup, we're doing this together, until the end," Reggie said.

"It's good to see you two bonding," Ebony said.

"Well, there's something about being a reporter that makes you want to get to the bottom of every story. I'm just not sure where to go from here," I said.

"It's simple, really," Olivia said. "When I'm preparing for a starring role on the stage, I do a lot of research. You two are in luck because the people you're researching are alive and well. Some of my most memorable characters were entirely made up. You have to observe these suspects of yours in their natural element to really know what motivates them. Do your research."

"How do we do that?" Reggie asked. "We can't stalk them."

"I've got it!" I shouted. Everyone stared at me. Maybe yelling wasn't the best approach, but I had a great idea. "You're going to take me out tomorrow, Reggie."

"That's a bit forward," Reggie said. "Do you have a specific place in mind?"

"We're going to a funeral," I said. "We're going to the funeral of Arthur Jones. As Olivia so eloquently suggested, let's see what makes these people really tick."

CHAPTER 13
ARTHUR JONES'S FUNERAL

I am always confused as to what to wear. So many women obsess about their clothes, and I'm one of them. It's not because I am a very fashion-forward person, it's just that I want to make a certain impression. I want to come across as smart and occasion-appropriate. I just don't want to be out of place and stick out.

Given that I was off to a funeral, wearing something dark was the obvious choice. My outfit had to be black or navy blue. So I searched my closet and found two pantsuits I thought would work. I threw them both across the bed when Majesta pounced. She was clearly upset at me. I don't think she fully recovered from me leaving her to go visit the neighbors last night.

I grabbed her and started to pet her soft, furry ear. She liked that. I could hear her purring loudly. Majesta was clearly saying, "Okay, maybe I will forgive you for leaving me here alone if you keep scratching my ear like that."

"I know you like that, baby, but I really have to get dressed before Reggie gets here," I said.

"But you still haven't fed me," Majesta chided.

"I totally forgot, baby. Let me stop everything I'm doing here and feed you," I said sarcastically. Regardless, I had to deal with Majesta or

I wasn't going to get anything done. In a lot of ways, I think I was Majesta's pet and not the other way around. Calico cats are known for their attitude, or cat-itude, as many describe it. Her breed is known for being very demanding and independent. Having said that, she is also very affectionate. Majesta is the best companion I could ask for. She keeps me thinking, grounded, and alert.

As I went downstairs to get her food, she followed lovingly. She also looked a little full of herself to me, almost as if she won an argument and I was now doing what she wanted me to do all along—to stop getting dressed and to feed her. If that was her goal all along, she surely was getting what she wanted this time.

I got in the black pantsuit just in time to hear the front doorbell ring. Reggie was also in a black suit. We both looked the part. My fears of looking out of place were unfounded for sure.

I had a pot of coffee just made, so I decided to share it with Reggie before we embarked. "Do you want some coffee?" I asked.

"Sure, I'd love some, Dimples," Reggie replied. "I have some things to ask you anyway, so this will be a good excuse for us to talk a bit."

"Really, what's on your mind?" I asked.

"I was looking through your online magazine. You call it *The News Sleuth*, right?"

"Yup, that's my magazine."

"It seems to be made up of essays written by people around the world discussing global news stories and trends."

"Right again. Where is this conversation going?"

"It seems weird to me that a former crime reporter would start a magazine that analyzes world news. Why not do something more in your lane?"

"I think we all have an obligation to search out the bigger trends, hence the addition of the word *sleuth* in the magazine title."

"I guess you are right, but why only talk about bigger news stories? Local news is very important too."

"Covering small crimes left me longing for more. I always wanted to cover the bigger stories, but the bigger crime stories, like murders, were never given to me. I guess they never trusted me with those stories. So I was always in search of the bigger story. I wanted more."

"That all makes sense, but now that you're in charge, you can really cover whatever you want to cover. Local stories can be very compelling. You could be writing about the death of Arthur Jones."

"I guess you're right. I never thought about it that way."

"Maybe you can start local sections of *The News Sleuth*? I could even write your entertainment section."

"Is that what this is all about?" I asked.

"What do you mean?" Reggie responded, confused.

"Are you looking for a job?" I asked.

"Of course not, but if you were offering, I would certainly consider it." Reggie smiled.

It was very flattering that Reggie wanted to work for me. I have to admit, I like being around him. But it never occurred to me to expand the magazine and take on more staff bloggers. I like working with just an in-person copy editor and a bunch of remote freelancers I never have to see face-to-face. I don't want to deal with a large, regular staff. I don't want to be forced to be in a position like Duke, where I have to crush the dreams of a new reporter looking for that big story. I can't see myself in that role.

"It's just something to think about," Reggie said.

"I really appreciate the suggestion. I will give it some real thought," I said. We finished our coffee and left for the funeral of Arthur Jones. Hopefully, we would discover more about why he died and who was behind it.

The funeral was not well attended. It was quite small. We saw Shanice, Yolanda, Tom, the preacher, and one other woman standing by Yolanda's side. Tom's arm was tight around Shanice, who was obviously crying. Yolanda was stoic, as always. She stood still and straight.

Reggie and I walked over to pay our respects and observe. We were welcomed politely by Shanice, who introduced us to everyone, including Eugenia, Yolanda's best friend, apparently. Eugenia was short and a bit plump, but very pleasant. Her smile was wide, and her cheeks were round. She wore a black dress with white polka dots throughout.

The preacher delivered a great talk. He was obviously close with the family. He talked about Arthur's childhood. He also talked about how close Arthur was to Eugenia, whom he called his aunt even though she was just a family friend. I think it was a good idea to attend, but we certainly were not learning anything new. This seemed like a typical funeral that a small family would hold for a lost loved one.

As things were about to conclude, in stepped DA Clarence and Lieutenant Crooks. Why were the DA and the police lieutenant here? That was not normal operating procedure.

"Why are you two here?" I asked.

"Is this really the time for your annoying questions?" Crooks shot back.

"Sheila is a solid reporter. I'm sure it's an occupational hazard," Clarence noted. "We could ask you the same thing, Sheila."

"I'm here to pay my respects, of course," I said.

"So are we," replied Crooks.

"I saw this man murdered, and we have to find out who did it!" I added.

"We are looking into it," Crooks said.

"But the evidence points to a robbery right now," Clarence interrupted.

"Robbers don't dress up like police," I said.

"I think we should all respect the family," Reggie said.

Shanice greeted Clarence and Crooks. She told them how sad she was and how the family has been hurting so much. "It's been a very hard time for us," Shanice said. "We appreciate you all stopping by to pay your respects, but it really was not necessary."

"We just wanted to follow up and see how you were doing," Clarence said. "We would be happy to accompany you back to your house."

"That's not necessary either," Tom said. "I'll be taking her home, and there are no other services. Arthur was a private man. He didn't want a lot of fuss. Perhaps Yolanda wants your assistance."

"Not at all," Yolanda snapped. "I'm going home to my house by myself. Thank you for coming, Eugenia. You are a true friend. You've listened to my darkest secrets and shared in my happiest moments. I love you, girl."

Yolanda hugged Eugenia close and left without addressing anyone else. She walked off with her head held high. The hug was almost shocking to me, after everything we had observed about her. It was so human, yet she always seemed so robotic. Now Eugenia was tearing up.

"He was a wonderful boy," Eugenia said. "He was such a joy to be around, especially when he had an idea or a dream to share. He lifted you up with his words and thoughts for sure."

"He was a good husband," Shanice added.

"I'm sure he was. Where is his father?" asked Clarence.

"He never knew his father. Yolanda told him his father died in a plane crash on his way to a conference for work. He was a world-class salesman. Yolanda described him as a proud immigrant who made a success of himself in America. She was very fond of him, from what I gathered hearing her talk about him," Shanice reported.

"I think that's enough for one day," Tom said. The two of them left together, hand in hand.

"It's a huge loss for the family," Eugenia said, and she turned to catch up to Shanice and Tom.

Crooks turned to me with a stern look. "You have some nerve coming here," he said to me.

"Why? I'm not the one making up some robbery story to quickly close this case. I'm looking for real answers," I said.

"I think this family needs some peace. We have to be discreet in conducting our investigation. It will be hard to find these robbers or whatever they are," Clarence said. "I don't want to disrupt this good family any more than we have to. We've looked hard at the police force, and we can't find anything. We have to put everything into perspective, Sheila. As you know, many robberies and murders go unsolved. We all have to be prepared for that eventuality here."

"I'm very aware of the statistics," I said.

Crooks and Clarence left together.

I turned to Reggie. "That was so weird."

"What's weird?" Reggie asked.

"I've covered a lot of crimes in this town, and I've never seen Crooks and Clarence take such an active role. They never go to funerals, and if they do, it's not for a nobody like Arthur Jones. Nobody knows who Arthur Jones is outside of his inner circle. He is not a celebrity or dignitary. It all just strikes me as being very, very odd."

"I guess so," Reggie said. "But if we look at this funeral as a whole, I would not say we learned a lot. It surely wasn't a waste of time, but I wouldn't say we broke the case wide open either."

Reggie was right, for sure, but we did learn some new things that made me think. I was still convinced Yolanda was hiding something big, and we also learned Arthur's father was killed when he was a baby. Also, Eugenia was a nice addition to the landscape of interesting people that were somehow involved with Arthur Jones and his not-quite-normal family.

"What did we learn?" I asked.

"Yolanda still seems very stoic," Reggie answered. "Looking at her is worth it. Shanice seems like the typical grieving widow. I'm not sure it's worth talking to her anymore unless we have something new to ask. She's been through a lot. I think we should leave her in peace for now."

"I agree," I said. "The new person in the picture is Eugenia. She seems very close to Yolanda, and it seems like she was very close to Arthur too. I think she's our next stop."

"I agree, but we don't know where she lives," Reggie said.

"That's no big deal, we'll just follow her home. You can tail her, right?" I asked with a smile.

CHAPTER 14
THE CHASE

Picture it: me in the passenger seat of a convertible with my hair blowing in the wind as we chase down the criminal. The car is weaving in and out of each lane to keep up. I look over at Reggie, with his curly, brown hair and his beautiful eyes as he intently guides us on this high-speed car chase. I should be scared, but I know it's all going to turn out fine in the end. I'm enjoying the ride as we just miss hitting the car in front of us as we swerve to match the speed of Eugenia. It's all so glamorous. It's all so exciting. It's exhilarating.

Well, none of that is happening, at least in the real world.

Eugenia drives like a snail. I can't imagine driving so slowly. We'll be following this woman forever. And she makes so many stops. We stopped at the grocery store, the dry cleaners, and now she is on the road again. If you want to catch a murderer, I guess you have to be patient and follow every lead.

The one thing in my little fantasy that is true is the role Reggie played. He's not going to let Eugenia get out of our sight. He is focused. He looks like his spine is permanently bent, he is so intently sitting forward in his chair. He's looking straight ahead with such concentration. Maybe too much concentration. Come to think of it, I hope he doesn't get a sore back or a stiff neck. I have to break the ice and make him more relaxed.

"How do you think this is going?" I asked.

"We're going to get to the bottom of it all," Reggie answered with determination.

"You don't have to do this with me."

"I know, but I want to. We're going to get this done, Dimples."

"You hardly know me, and you're all wrapped up in this with me."

"We're neighbors; I'm being neighborly."

He certainly was that. Who would have thought the new neighbor I almost ran over when he was moving in next door would be so nice? Sometimes the best partnerships start from the craziest encounters, I guess. We're part Bonnie and Clyde and part Abbott and Costello. Well, regardless of how you characterize us, we're a team. In the end, it doesn't matter what we're like, just that we are.

"You can calm down, you know," I assured him.

"I'm very calm!" he shouted. "We are not going to lose her!"

"I don't think that's possible; she's going, like, twenty miles an hour."

Reggie sighed. I said too much. I was too critical. Time to change the subject.

"What got you into theater writing?" I asked.

"I'm a failed actor; what else was I going to do? Why did you start your online publication?" Reggie asked.

"I'm a failed news reporter. I worked for a paper, but they never trusted me to cover the real news. I guess I was never fulfilled as a crime reporter that covered petty theft. I always wanted the bigger stories but never got them. I was always looked over. I always felt judged a little. So I just started my own publication, and it's been enough to sustain me financially. I also got to employ my best friend, Tania, as my copy editor, so it's all worked out. I guess I finally got what I wished for. Here I am tracking down a real murder."

"I guess that's good, but you do know your publication is not complete," Reggie noted as if to tease me about what it was missing.

"What do you mean?" I asked in a very hurt, angry tone.

"I don't mean to pass further judgement on you or your work, but your publication doesn't include an entertainment section. It's all news analysis."

"I suppose you're right. I never valued entertainment, I guess."

"Coming from a woman that never felt valued professionally herself, maybe you should expand your horizons a bit. Think outside of the box. Offer your readers a fuller picture of the world. We all need to be entertained from time to time. Like I told you, I may be inclined to write it if you pull that trigger."

I guess entertainment has value, I thought. It must. It's big business, after all. But right now was not the time for a bigger conversation about the benefits of TV or movies or theater or whatever else people do to entertain themselves. Eugenia was about to make another stop, this time at the pharmacy.

The car screeched to a halt. I was jerked forward. I felt my face headed straight for the windshield, but Reggie helped me. I felt his arm come across me. He braced me. He saved me. I went from feeling so nervous to feeling so comforted, so safe. Reggie did that for me, and it was a nice feeling. It was a foreign feeling for me, but a nice feeling, to be sure.

"Stay in your lane!" Reggie shouted.

Some car darted in front of us. Given that we were going so slow, it would have been fine, but Reggie stomped on the brake. He's even a bit dramatic in how he operates a car, but that's okay. That was all okay with me.

"Sorry if I scared you," he said.

"Not at all," I responded as I stared into his eyes. He didn't notice the stare because he was so focused on the road, which is probably for the best.

Eugenia pulled into the parking lot of the pharmacy, and we followed. Reggie saw her leave her car and he immediately reached into his back seat. He was throwing and tossing things here and there. When he returned upright to his front seat, he was wearing aviator sunglasses and a hat commonly seen on a private detective in a 1950s film noir movie.

"I'm going after her, baby," he said. "You wait here, I'll be right back."

He darted out of the car and ran for the pharmacy. I had to laugh. That didn't just happen. I took it in and quickly realized it did happen, so I laughed some more.

With Reggie in the pharmacy, I guessed this was a good time to do some snooping. I was going to check out the back seat. Wow! I didn't realize how much stuff he had lying around back there. It was like a costume shop. He had sunglasses and hats and leather pants. I just saw something pink popping out of the seat as I looked from side to side. This is just unreal. I tugged on the pink object only to find it just grew and grew longer and longer as I pulled more and more. It was a feather boa. This was just too much. I couldn't help it; I had to laugh some more.

At that moment, I happened to be looking outside the car, and I spotted Eugenia. She was looking very annoyed as she left the pharmacy and went to her car. You could just see the anger in her face. I wondered what happened. Then Reggie came running to the car, holding his back in pain. This was not going to be good.

"Are you okay?" I asked. "You look like you are in pain, Reggie."

"I fell," he replied.

"How?" I inquired.

"Well, I was following Eugenia real close; too close. I didn't realize the floor was wet. I got too caught up in it all. I didn't see the wet floor sign at all. Just as she was checking out, I slipped, fell straight on my back, and took the display of lipsticks down with me."

"I'm so sorry," I was working overtime not to laugh yet again. It was all too funny. But there was no time for jokes. Eugenia was driving off, so Reggie went back into car-chase mode and drove off behind her.

We were on the hunt again. Hopefully, this time she would just go home so we could talk to her. I knew she knew what happened. Okay, maybe she doesn't know *exactly* what happened, but I am convinced she knows something. I have to find out what she knows.

On the road, Reggie started to open up about his past. He told me about the joys of being a theater actor and moving an audience. All those things in the back seat came from past performances. Now he writes about theater mostly. Maybe I was wrong, but he seems unsatisfied. He doesn't seem excited about his writing.

I liked having him around. I was so used to it just being me and Tania. Ever since college it'd been just the two of us, hanging out and conquering the challenges of this crazy world as they come our way. Reggie is a perfect addition. It's like he's always been there, really.

Now Eugenia was pulling into a Wal-Mart. Will this woman ever stop shopping? This time, I volunteer to go in. "You wait here this time; I'll go in," I tell Reggie. I grab a glittery pair of sunglasses and follow her in.

Eugenia looks at the dresses. I am right there behind her. She moves to the grocery section. I am following her. She moves to the shoe section. I am sticking close, but then I feel a tap on my shoulder. I jump in fear. I don't know why I'm afraid. I'm in Wal-Mart, for goodness's sake. I guess it's all this skulking around.

I turn around to see who it is—you guessed it, it's Reggie.

"I thought you would stay in the car this time," I said.

"And let you have all the fun? No way, Dimples," Reggie says. "Try this on."

He handed me a blue Wal-Mart employee vest. I noticed he was wearing one too.

"Where did you get these?"

"Don't worry about it, Dimples. We need to blend in better."

I reluctantly put the vest on and keep following Eugenia. Then I feel the tap on my shoulder again. I don't jump. I'm not afraid. It's just Reggie again. I turn around and a big guy has Reggie by the collar and a bigger guy is staring at me. This is serious!

"Those are our vests," the larger man says.

We are in trouble now. How do we get out of this one? What a pickle. We have to act. So I take off the vest and throw it in the guy's face and run for my life. Reggie follows suit, and we are both headed for the door. The adrenaline is pumping. I can see the sliding doors in front of me. We are so close to getting out of this Wal-Mart.

Then, it happens. I slip on the floor as I am running. On the way down, I grab Reggie to regain my balance and he goes down too. We both fall into the cereal display and before we know it, we are on the floor covered in Cheerios and Fruity Pebbles. How embarrassing! Before, I compared us to a mix of Bonnie and Clyde and Abbott and Costello. I take it back; we're just Abbott and Costello. In my haste to get out of the store, I did not see the wet floor sign. Now I know how Reggie felt in the pharmacy.

Thankfully, everyone at the store was very understanding. They let us leave without any further issues.

"Who didn't see the wet floor sign this time?" Reggie said to me with a smile.

I smacked him jokingly, and we both laughed as we got back to his car. Our luck wasn't all bad because we saw Eugenia getting in her car at the exact same time. The chase was on again. Thankfully, it looked like she was driving toward a residential area this time. Eugenia pulled in a driveway and we pulled a little way past it to the curb and parked.

"That was a close call," I told Reggie.

"A good costume goes a long way toward creating a character, even if it is someone else's costume," Reggie noted.

"Where did you learn that?"

"At Julliard."

"I guess I can't argue with that, but next time, let's not steal anything, okay?"

Just then, we heard a loud knock on the driver's side window. This time we both jumped in fear. We didn't realize Eugenia had walked over to our car, which was now parked near the sidewalk. What should we do? Reggie took charge and rolled down the window to address her, but she spoke up before he could say anything.

"Do you two want to come inside so we can talk?" she asked.

"That sounds great, actually," Reggie responded in a confused voice.

"Why the confusion in your tone? I'm a Black woman in America, I know when a white woman is following me. Besides, you two weren't exactly inconspicuous about it."

I guess we weren't. All the falling and wrecking the stores must have given us away, I thought. No matter; we were going to get that conversation after all, so that's what counts.

As we walked into her house, it was easy to see she was a spiritual woman. She had crosses hanging on the walls and many family pictures. This was the house of a good woman.

"What do you want to know?" she asked us.

"What do you know about Arthur and his family?" I asked.

"Arthur was like a son to me. Yolanda was always working, so I was often taking care of Arthur. His passing is so tragic. Do you really think he was targeted for murder?"

"Who told you that?" Reggie responded.

"Yolanda, of course. At least, that's what she thinks you guys think. Yolanda loved Arthur. Of course, she loved her work more, but what can you do? She worked for a lot of high-powered lawyers, and she was always in the office."

"I bet," Reggie said mockingly.

I elbowed him. We didn't want to upset Eugenia.

"No worries, sweetie. It's okay," Eugenia told me. "Yolanda did have a lot of boyfriends. There was one in particular she talked about all the time. She never told me his name, just that he was a hard-working immigrant who became who he was because of the goodness of America. She said he often compared our country to an onion. He said it's dark and ugly when you first see it, with all the skin and stuff, but once you peel back the layers you see a beautiful center that tastes amazing. I think that man was Arthur's father, but I never asked. She never even told me his name."

"What happened to him?" I asked.

"He passed recently. Yolanda was very upset about it. She turned to Arthur for support, and Arthur seemed to be plotting his next move."

Well, there you have it. I heard Yolanda yelling at Arthur on the phone that morning. The plan must have gone wrong and she had to get rid of him. But would someone really do that to their child? Probably not, but Yolanda would. I never saw her cry throughout this whole thing, not once.

On our way out, Eugenia stopped us.

"Do you know why Yolanda named her son Arthur?" she asked. We both shook our heads no. "Her mom was obsessed with Camelot. She told Yolanda the story often. Yolanda said Arthur was her Excalibur, so that's why she called him Arthur."

"One more tiny question," I said. "Are you sure Yolanda loved her son?"

Eugenia didn't answer, she just led us to the door politely. That seals it, I thought. She always saw Arthur as her meal ticket, even as a baby. She was the murderer for sure; now I just had to prove it.

CHAPTER 15
GOING UNDERCOVER

As we pulled up to Reggie's house, we saw Tania sitting on the stoop in front of my house's front door. I totally forgot about Tania. I totally forgot about work, real work, like putting out my publication. Who needs work anyway when you have a murder to get to the bottom of? We all have priorities, I guess.

Nonetheless, we all have to be responsible. It sounds lame, but it's true. I could see the disappointment on Tania's face. She looked mad. She was about to give me a hard time. I knew she was going to scold me like you would not believe about abandoning the publication like I did today.

Reggie and I looked at each other with a bit of shame in our glances as we left the car and walked toward Tania. As we calmly walked, she got up and ran to us. I thought she was going to pounce. I even closed my eyes. The smackdown was coming my way and I deserved it.

In that moment, I did something unexpected. This was new to me, but it seemed so natural. I grabbed Reggie's hand and squeezed it for comfort to lighten the blow. Who would have thought? I guess I had come to trust Reggie. What was also great was that he didn't resist. He let me squeeze his hand as Tania got closer and closer. She was literally up in my face when she started to talk.

"How did it go?" she asked in a very excited voice.

I was shocked. She wasn't upset that I was out with Reggie while she was home waiting and waiting for me. If I were her, I think I would have been pissed off.

"It went well. Reggie wrecked the pharmacy, and we both almost got arrested at the Wal-Mart, but we did get some good information. I feel like it was all worth it," I answered.

"Let's go in the house and decide what's next," Reggie said smartly.

Once in the house, I was greeted by my bossy cat, Majesta. She was scratching at my leg. It became uncomfortable, so I picked her up. I could sense her displeasure with me. She looked me straight in the face as I held her up.

"You did not feed me this morning!" she scolded me.

"I know, I'm sorry," I responded.

"Who are you talking to, Dimples?" Reggie asked.

I responded that I was talking to nobody and quickly went into the kitchen to feed Majesta. Tania and Reggie went into the living room together. I could tell Reggie was eager to tell Tania about our adventures and all we learned from Eugenia. It was nice to see the two of them becoming fast friends. Tania can be very judgmental.

When I went into the living room, the two of them quickly straightened up. That was not good. Tania gets very formal when she has a crazy plan or idea or thought. I was bracing myself for what I was about to hear as I slowly sat down on the sofa.

"Reggie told me about your little adventure," she said.

"Yes, it has been quite a day," I responded.

"It seems so," she noted.

"It was," I said.

"Well, good for you two," she said encouragingly.

"Thanks." I knew it was coming.

She leaned forward intently on the sofa and I closed my eyes to brace myself for what was about to come. "Reggie and I were talking, and we think I should apply to be Tom's new secretary. The other secretary did not work out. We know he's looking for a replacement, and we know he has some business or other connection to Yolanda.

We have to find out how those two are connected if we are ever going to get the proof we need to get Yolanda or whoever else killed Arthur. Before you object, you know this is the only way," Tania blurted out.

"What if they recognize you? This is a bad idea," I said in response to this harebrained plan, which I knew was coming, by the way.

"Tom has never seen me, and if others recognize me, I'll just say you fired me and I needed a job," Tania begged.

"I don't think this is going to work, and who knows if he would even hire you," I countered.

"He'll hire me. I'll make sure of it," Tania said.

"It's a good plan. We need something to pin this on Yolanda aside from a hunch, Dimples. This is our best bet," Reggie interrupted.

I knew we couldn't go to the police with what we had because, face it, we had nothing. This was a horrible idea, but we had to give it a try. "Okay, go for it," I said begrudgingly.

"Great!" Tania cried.

"We're going undercover," said Reggie.

"The two of you are too dramatic," I said.

All three of us laughed, and Tania quickly left to go see Tom. She was excited, and she didn't want to waste any time. Reggie and I agreed we would wait here in my house for her to return so she could quickly report back on how things went.

Some time had passed since Tania left. It seemed like hours, but it'd probably been just a few minutes. Reggie and I sat in the living room, staring at each other. Neither of us talking, just staring. Okay, this needed to end. So I offered to make us some iced tea. He agreed, so I left him there to go to the kitchen.

I am no master chef. I can cook a bit, but nothing to write home about. Cooking is fun, don't get me wrong, I just never took the time to really perfect my culinary skills. But even I can't screw up iced tea, right? So I reached for the water in the fridge and the iced tea mix. All you do is pour the water in the cup, add the mix, and stir; how hard can it be?

I reached for the cups, poured the water, and Majesta jumped on the counter next to me. For whatever reason, the sudden movement scared me, so I jumped forward and I hit both cups into the sink. Great, now Miss Clumsy will have to start all over again.

"You forget to feed me and now you're making him iced tea?" Majesta sneered.

"Don't be jealous," I responded in kind.

"Whatever," Majesta retorted as she jumped off the counter.

This time I was successful in making the iced tea, and I turned to take the cups to the living room when I saw Reggie standing there and, you guessed it, I dropped the cups yet again, only this time their contents decorated my kitchen floor instead of the sink.

Reggie quickly bent down to help me clean up. "Who were you talking to?" he asked.

I looked at Majesta, now in the corner of the room looking at me. I could swear I saw her smirk in delight. "Nobody, just myself, I guess," I quickly responded.

We gathered our thrice-made drinks and went back to the living room. Hopefully, I could get to the sofa without dropping my drink again. Woo-hoo! We made it back to the sofa spill-free.

"Sorry, I am a bit clumsy," I said, blushing a bit.

"I noticed. I still have fond memories of the day I moved in next door," he said.

"Very funny. You could have said something like: I didn't notice," I pointed out.

There was a second of silence, and then we both started laughing. I feel so easy with Reggie. He's so normal and he gets me for some reason. I've only felt that way with Tania. People are often turned off by my clumsiness and the fact that I'm always asking questions. I guess I am what is commonly called an acquired taste.

Reggie seemed familiar. He was comfortable. I just like being around him and talking and wrecking Wal-Marts. You know, the simple things in life everyone enjoys. Also, he listens, and he seems to value what I say. He doesn't dismiss me or talk down to me. Maybe he's just acting; after all, he is an actor turned writer. It could all just be a cover for how he really feels about me. Maybe he is just humoring me. When you think about it, anything is possible, I guess. Who cares though? I should just enjoy the company, right? If he is playing me for some unknown reason, at least I'm enjoying the ride for now.

Once again, he pitched me on adding an entertainment section to my publication instead of just focusing solely on news analysis. Maybe that's what he wants. He just wants to write a section of my publication. That has to be it.

As he was about to plead his case, the doorbell rang. It was Tania; she's back. Hopefully, everything went well.

She looked happy. She looked very happy. Tania is not discreet. You can see her true feelings all over her face. You will never guess how many fortune tellers and psychics have scammed her. Poor Tania was an easy mark.

"I take it everything went well," I said.

"I can never hide anything from you," Tania replied.

"Tell us what happened," Reggie said eagerly.

That was never the best thing to say to Tania. Reggie didn't know it, but he just opened the floodgates of Tania's imagination. She loves to tell stories, especially stories where she is the star. But I guess actors like to hear stories, so this might work out for all involved. Tania can tell one of her tall tales, Reggie can enjoy the telling, and I can sit back and listen intently.

Tania explained how she entered Tom's office and quickly whisked him off his feet. She said he was one hundred percent into her the minute she knocked at his front office door. Who knows, maybe that part was true. She told him she types two hundred words per minute. I had to stop her.

"Did you really say that?" I asked.

"Of course I did," Tania replied.

"You do know the average person types fifty words per minute?" I noted.

"Everyone is entitled to a few dramatic liberties," Reggie said. "Go on, what happened next?"

Tania explained how she dazzled him with her shorthand and her clerical abilities. I know Tania. Tania does not know shorthand, and her clerical abilities are better described as comical. This was not going well. Reading between the lines, I was waiting for the big letdown because this tale was obviously going nowhere fast.

"So did he hire you?" I asked.

"Always with the questions," Tania said. "Can't I just tell you what happened next?"

"Did he hire you?" I asked again, ever so politely.

"Well, not exactly," Tania said.

"I knew it. This was a bad idea," I said.

"Not exactly," Tania noted. "He said he would call me."

"Did you give him a resume or a list of references?" I asked.

"Not exactly, I just wrote my number on a piece of paper with my lipstick and gave it to him," Tania reported. "Now we just have to wait."

Reggie could sense I was not convinced he would call. "Sometimes people hire based on feelings and connections. Did he ask you for a resume or recommendations?"

"Nope," Tania said. "He was too busy looking down my shirt, which is why I thought giving him my number with the lipstick would be just the ticket."

"Great thinking!" Reggie shouted.

Reggie appreciated the theatrics, as I thought, and Tania surely delivered. She was a woman of action that could think quickly on her feet. She knew what Tom wanted, so she delivered. That's why I like her. I could never do that. I'd have asked so many questions about the job he would have thrown me out of his office in no time.

I guess it went as well as we could have expected. Surely Tom was not going to hire her on the spot. These things take time. I remembered how many rounds of interviews I had to go through before the paper would hire me. It was exhausting. Every time I thought I had the job, they would call me to tell me someone else had to meet with me first. I met with the associate editor, the editor, and the publisher. It was so stressful. I really wanted that job. I wanted to be on the streets covering the latest homicides, grilling the police officers, questioning the DA.

As they say, be careful what you wish for. I got the job, but I never got to cover the stories I dreamed of. Some things are just not meant to be, I guess. Some things are just not what they are cracked up to be. We sometimes create a fantasy in our heads we just can't attain, or at least I do anyway. Fantasies aren't bad. It's good to indulge in a healthy fantasy from time to time. We all need an escape.

Tania's cell phone rang. She quickly answered. Tania said, "Hello," sweetly and listened for a while. After that, she responded by saying, "Of course," and hung up.

"Well, who was that?" Reggie asked intently.

"Tell us," I added enthusiastically.

"I'm hired," Tania said with a huge smile. "We're in. I'm going undercover."

CHAPTER 16

SOMETHING STRANGE IS GOING ON

The next morning began on a note of introspection for me. Good for Tania, I thought. She got the job. Tania has always been one to get her way. She makes her own fate. Me, I let fate make me. I let myself be guided. I think. I methodically follow things to their next logical step. I don't skip ahead. I listen to the rules. I pay attention. I ask probing questions. Maybe that's why Tania and I get along so well. She complements me. Tania is a finished person, whereas I am very much still a work in progress, searching for the next thing, longing to cover the hard-hitting news as only I can.

Reggie and I are similar, I think. We both longed for another path— me as a homicide reporter, and him as a famous actor—but instead we turned into analysis writers. All in all, I thought we make the perfect team.

Majesta jumped on the bed beside me and looked me straight in the eyes. She was determined to get my attention. "You aren't going to forget to feed me again this morning, right?" she asked pointedly.

"Of course not," I responded politely.

Majesta rubbed her head lovingly across my cheek. She was certainly bossy, but she was also very loving.

With that little nudge, I went down to the kitchen to feed her. See what I mean about being guided? I can't help it.

Today would be my first day without Tania. I still had a publication to put out, even though my copy editor was posing as a secretary to get the goods on a possible murderer. I just knew it would be a lonely day. I was going to have to do everything myself.

Then, it came to me: no, I won't. I am going to march next door and see if Reggie will help me while Tania is otherwise engaged. Sometimes the best ideas come to me in the morning, after feeding Majesta.

So I got myself dressed and ready and go over to Reggie's house. I rang the doorbell and, fortunately, he answered right away.

"It's too early for news from Tania," he said.

"I haven't heard from her yet, but I was wondering if you might help me," I asked.

"But of course, my fair lady. Please come in, Dimples." He bowed and gestured, leading me in his house. Dramatic as ever.

I stepped in and quickly tripped. My face was headed for his hardwood floors, but he caught me before that could be my fate. There I was in his arms, staring into his eyes. Just clumsy Sheila at it again. Who falls when entering someone's house? Just me, that's who. Fortunately for me, Reggie should be used to it by now, so I'm not so embarrassed.

"Sorry about that," he said as he let me go. "There's a step down right after entering the front door. I don't know why the builder did that. I have to get that fixed for sure."

See what I mean? He was making excuses for me. He knows me. Hopefully, he'd agree to be my copy editor until Tania comes back. It's not writing a theater or entertainment section, like he desired, but it's something. Regardless, he still had his theater column, so maybe he would be willing to take this other assignment on for me.

"I was wondering if you would be my copy editor until Tania comes back," I asked longingly.

"I thought you'd never ask," he responded enthusiastically.

He agreed! Success! Maybe this day wasn't going to be as lonely as I first imagined.

"You will have to go easy on me, Dimples. I'm used to being the writer that gets edited, not the other way around," he added.

"It's easy. You'll be great. Also, I'm sure Tania will be back shortly. How long could this undercover thing go anyway?" I pointed out.

"I've just been hired and already you can't wait for me to go," Reggie said with a chuckle. He seemed very excited to work with me. Maybe a bit too excited, if you ask me. Nonetheless, I was not going to complain. I woke up this morning thinking I was going to have to put out my entire publication myself, and now I had much-needed help.

"So what do we do first?" he asked.

"I don't know. Tania usually doesn't show up until ten or so," I responded.

"So what do you do before she gets to work? Every writer has a tried-and-true routine," he added.

"I used to go to Harry's to get a bagel, but since the incident, I haven't gone as much," I confessed.

"Well, you're going today," he commanded. Reggie picked up his jacket and pushed me out the door. It was sweet how he was trying to get me back into my routines.

The minute we arrived at Harry's, we were greeted by a new server. She was young, probably in her twenties, with short, brown hair and deep-red highlights. Maybe it was just me judging based on appearance but she looked very smart, very bohemian, very avant-garde.

Once Harry came out front, he was quick to come over and greet us. "My dear Sheila. I am so happy to see you again, my friend. We have been missing you. You don't come around as often," he said.

"She will be coming around as usual," Reggie responded.

Harry's eyes lit up. He hugged Reggie tightly and then he hugged me. After that, he turned to the new server.

"This is my daughter, Jessica. She is a senior in college. She just finished her internship with the DA, and she is helping me out today," Harry said proudly.

"It's a pleasure to meet you," I said. "Getting an internship with the DA is a very big deal. You must be very proud of her, Harry. How did you like working with Clarence?"

"You know him?" Jessica asked.

"Sort of," I said. "I analyze the news and I was a crime reporter, so we've come into contact enough times for him to know me and for me to know him."

"He's good, I guess. He is very preoccupied with his campaign for governor, and he has been very impacted by his father's passing," Jessica reported.

"I'm sure Mr. Family Values will be just fine," Harry said sarcastically. "I would never have imagined my daughter would be a political science major. When she was a child, we would cook together. She loves food. She is definitely a foodie. She used to collect recipes. As a young girl, she told me it made her relax."

"I'm not a little girl anymore, Dad, but I still like to cook. It is relaxing, and healing and comforting, all at the same time," Jessica countered. She looked behind me intently. "I think some people are looking for you."

It was my friends waving me over to a booth. There was Samantha, Oliver, Clark, and Leslie. This was going to be a real homecoming of sorts. I was quick to respond and brought Reggie over with me.

"These are my morning friends. This is Samantha. She is so intuitive, and she loves DC Comics. She also heads up our neighborhood's bank. This is Oliver. I've known him the longest, and he is a Marvel fan. He is our fire chief. Our newer members are Clark and Leslie. Clark is an English teacher."

"That's me, an Asian English teacher," Clark said as he reached out his hand to shake Reggie's.

"Isn't he so witty?" Leslie said adoringly. "I'm Sheila's friend Leslie. I work with the mayor. And who are you?"

"I'm Sheila's new neighbor, Reggie. I'm excited to meet everyone," Reggie answered kindly.

We all sat down, and Jessica came over to take our orders. I told everyone how I fantasize about Harry's amazing bagels. Jessica responded by sharing her own fantasy to someday visit Alaska.

"The American author Tom Bodett quoted naturalist John Muir when he wrote in his journal that you should never go to Alaska as a young man because you'll never be satisfied with any other place as long as you live. I don't know about being too young to visit Alaska, but I do want to go. And maybe I'll take you all with me," Jessica said.

"You just met us," Sheila said.

"I can tell we are going to be fast friends," Jessica proudly asserted.

"I've missed our morning talks," I said to the group.

"And we've missed you too," Samantha replied.

"I knew you'd be back. Look at how many people have donned the Captain America shield, but the good-old Captain America always comes back," Oliver explained. He just couldn't resist slipping a Marvel reference in there.

"In the end, I think we all have to go back to where we started in order to move forward," Clark added.

"That's so insightful," Leslie admired.

It was a very telling thing to say. I knew that, after all the pleasantries and good food, I would have to check out the alley again. Maybe I would remember something new. Maybe being there again would jog my memory and bring back more.

Time passed. It was a blast reconnecting with everyone. I looked down at my watch and noticed it was almost eleven o'clock. Clark had left to go to class a while back, and Leslie left shortly thereafter, as always. I told Samantha and Oliver we had to go. On the way out, I said good-bye to Harry and his daughter, Jessica.

"Reggie, we have to go to the alley," I said.

"I figured you would want another look, Dimples," Reggie said. "I think it will also help if you talk things through with me. What did Arthur seem like to you? What do you remember exactly?"

"He was dressed very formally. He had on a suit and tie. He was clearly gearing up for an important event of some kind. Arthur seemed normal. He talked to his wife and told her he was about to back out of something with Tom because he had a bigger deal in the works. After that, his mother called. She must have been upset about something because Arthur was reassuring her of the bright future ahead. Little did he know."

"You can stop there if you want to take a moment," Reggie said, noticing my eyes were getting a bit red and watery.

"Nope, I have to keep going. It was the third call that was weird.

He was talking to someone as if they had invited him to meet at Harry's, but the person changed their mind. He called the person 'bro' and left in a huff. Of course, I followed him, and that's when I saw it all happen. It was shocking. It was horrible," I recalled.

"Look around the alley. Does anything new catch your eye?" Reggie asked.

"It was so quick, really. I just remember the woman's pink-tipped hair and her charm bracelet. I never saw her face. The man turned around to look at me, but I ran away. I noticed his big, brown beard and his cloudy, gray eye, but that's it. I ran for help, and when I got back with Harry and everyone, Arthur was dead and the two murderers were gone."

It started to rain. It wasn't a downpour or anything, it was a sun shower. I knew it would pass. The water was cool, very soothing on my face. It was very comforting, but it wasn't enough to stop the tears from flowing. I saw someone die in this alley. How could that be? Poor Arthur.

Reggie swooped me up and hugged me. He held me tight. Reggie knew it would come to this: me crying in this horrible alley and him comforting me. Some people might turn away, but he just came closer. Reggie was an empathetic man. Feelings were important to him, I could tell.

"It's okay," he said calmly. "We are going to figure out what happened here and why. Yolanda, or whoever, is not going to get away with killing Arthur. They say justice is always served."

"Maybe they say that in the theater or the movies, but I've seen many cases go unsolved, not that I ever got a chance to cover those cases, mind you," I responded. "This might fit into that category. We really don't have anything. We've done a lot of running around but we only have hunches and leads, no real facts."

"They'll come. We're not done yet, Dimples," Reggie said.

"Are you sure?" I asked.

"I'm positive."

Just then, my cell phone rang and rang. I was so busy pouring my heart out and hugging Reggie, I didn't even hear it. I sometimes zone out. I guess, under the circumstances, it's understandable. But, finally, I realized it was ringing, and I answered. It was Tania. She was excited, but Tania is always excited. I knew I was in for another grand story. I didn't know if I wanted to hear another Tania story right now, frankly. I needed this emotional release, and I was basking in it, quite frankly. It was just nice.

Tania was persistent, but unusually succinct. She got right to the point, and she was whispering so Tom didn't hear. I hung up the phone after acknowledging what she reported to me.

"Well, what did she say?" Reggie asked impatiently.

"She said something very strange is going on at Tom's office," I said. "Something very, very strange."

CHAPTER 17
PARTNERS IN CRIME

They always say the waiting is the hardest part, and they aren't wrong. What did Tania find out? What strange things were going on in Tom's office? Maybe she found the connection that would point us directly to Yolanda. Tania is very persuasive, God knows. Maybe this whole nightmare would be over soon. Maybe we'd get the evidence we needed to prove that a mother so cold, so unfeeling as Yolanda has appeared every time we've seen her, took it upon herself to have her own son killed. I knew it was hard to believe, but the way things were shaping up, I believed it.

What was taking Tania so long after all? We needed to hear what she meant exactly. Here me and Reggie were in the car parked across the street from Tom's office, just waiting. Tania said she would come out as soon as she could get away, and we were dutifully waiting for her grand entrance. Reggie was in the zone. He loved grand entrances, and he knew Tania would deliver. Reggie was a trained showman and Tania was a natural. Birds of a feather.

Reggie started singing the popular refrain from some Tom Petty song I can't remember. He sang, if you can call it singing, because he sounded more like he was screaming.

"Now I can see why you went into acting and not singing," I said jokingly.

"We all have our talents," Reggie noted. "Hopefully, Tania will be out soon. Until then, I have to admit, I am having fun with you, even if you have rejected my tender serenade."

"Tender is not the word I would use," I replied. "But the company is surely tender, and then some."

Suddenly, he leaned in toward me. I could feel his breath on my face. The heat of the moment started to flow within me. I closed my eyes. I was ready for the kiss. I was wanting the kiss. Then, he carefully took a stray eyelash off my cheek.

"It was just resting there, Dimples," Reggie said. "I had to move in a bit closer to get a good look. You probably didn't even notice that stray eyelash."

"No, I didn't," I responded, very disappointed.

"It would be a shame for my tenure as your copy editor to come to an end before it even really started," Reggie noted.

I was feeling the same way. Maybe the kiss was a bit premature, but, regardless, the company was so satisfying. Reggie's presence was calming and encouraging all at the same time. I hoped he felt the same way about me.

He was right, it would be a shame for our working partnership to end so soon. Either way, he was still going to be my neighbor. I had to focus on the positives because that's what I do in these sticky moments.

The back car door slammed shut and Reggie and I jumped. We were startled. What was going on? We both quickly looked in the back seat to see Tania there in the middle of all of Reggie's costume props. I guess the door was unlocked and she came in. Looking at her, I knew immediately she had something important to report, and Reggie knew it too.

"I thought you two would never notice I was back here," Tania said.

"What happened?" I asked.

"Yes, what did you find out?" Reggie asked.

"What's going on over there at Tom's?" I prodded.

"Always with the questions," Tania responded. "That's just it, nothing is going on. It's so weird."

"What do you mean exactly? You said something strange was going on," I said sharply. I was not in the mood for the buildup to something big, I had to know.

"I've been in that office all morning, and nothing has happened. No phone calls. No visitors. No work at all," Tania pointed out.

"Nothing?" I asked.

"Nothing at all. You can hear a pin drop in that office. But Tom sure is interested in me. He's been making small talk like you would not believe."

I was so sure we were going to find the smoking gun. I thought we were going to break this case wide open today. I guess the undercover antics were going to have to continue. We shouldn't give up yet. We knew Yolanda had business with Tom, and we had to find out what it is.

"Now what?" Reggie asked, confused. "Where do we go from here?"

"What do you mean?" Tania responded, insulted. "I'm not done here. I'm going to find out how he is making his money and what the connection is to Yolanda. I can't leave until I at least find out those two things, don't you think?"

"She's right," Reggie said.

"I agree," I agreed.

"Great! I was hoping we would all agree. Tom has asked me out to lunch. I think you guys should follow behind, but be discreet. Maybe I will get an opportunity to ask about his business. I have to keep digging. Nothing means something. There's more to what's going on in that office."

Tania wrote down the name and address of the restaurant and gave it to me before she left the car to go back to Tom. Tania was right; it was strange that nothing at all was going on. Tom did not seem desperate for business or money. He seemed like a successful businessman that fit right in with Arthur's family. I guessed time would tell.

We saw Tom and Tania come out of the office together and get in his car. We followed behind them, as they undoubtedly were off to lunch together. Answers had to come from this stakeout. Reggie and I were going to pay close attention to the conversation and see if we could get more leads to follow. My association with Reggie wasn't over yet. We were going to see this through together.

The restaurant Tom picked was nice. It served American food, so it wasn't fancy or anything, but it had nice outdoor seating overlooking a creek. My guess is the food wouldn't win any cooking awards, but who am I to judge? However, the atmosphere was right on. Looking at the creek while you eat was so peaceful. It was nothing short of serene. Tom knew what he was doing when he picked this spot. I wondered how many women he'd taken here.

Of course, he requested to eat outside. He knew the host by name. Again, not surprising. So Reggie and I followed. Reggie put on his aviators and a baseball cap this time. I grabbed a wide-brimmed black hat and dark, black sunglasses. He even had women's stuff in his back seat. I guess I shouldn't be too surprised. We requested to sit next to Tom and Tania, but not too close. We wanted to observe, but from a safe distance.

"Can you hear them from here?" I whispered.

"I think so," Reggie answered.

"By the way, why do you have women's stuff in your back seat?" I asked.

"An actor needs to be prepared for all kinds of roles," Reggie said with an air of confidence.

Tom was looking straight at Tania's cleavage. What a pig. He didn't even hide it. Men like that disgust me. But Tania knew what she was doing. She was laughing in a flirty way. That's my best friend, a resourceful, smart, confident woman. Reggie was leaning in to hear their conversation. It was too much. He was too much. They were going to notice him, so I slapped him on the knee to motion him to sit back.

"What are you doing?" Reggie asked.

"Lean in a little more and you'll fall over," I responded.

Tania was asking questions about the business, but she was being pitch perfect, not too inquisitive. I had to admit, her questions were good, but mine are better. However, she's not a journalist, so I can't judge her too harshly. Still, you'd think she would learn something from being around me so long.

Something changed. Tom straightened up. He saw someone or something. Maybe he recognized me. Did I blow it for Tania? I could hear him mention the name Yolanda, but I didn't get the context. *Now we're getting somewhere.* Tom stood up from his chair as if he was trying to greet someone. Tania also stood up. What was going on? What were they doing? Maybe Tom invited someone else to the lunch.

"Sheila, please," Reggie said. "Remember what you told me."

What was Reggie talking about? I know Tom said, "Yolanda." I had to hear the context. Shoot, I should be the one over there asking the questions.

My eyes widened as I looked forward. It was Yolanda. She was coming to sit with them. This was really it! This was the break we needed. Or maybe not.

"I know you," Yolanda said.

"What do you mean?" asked Tania.

"You're with that woman that said she saw my son die," Yolanda accused.

"What is going on here?" Tom asked.

"I can explain," Tania said. "I was her copy editor and she fired me. Can you believe it? She fired me! We were best friends. We met in college. I carried her. Nobody liked her."

"I can see how that would be the case," Yolanda responded.

Then, it happened. I fell on the floor. Reggie was trying to warn me I was leaning in too much, just like he was when I warned him, but it was too late. I was on the floor, completely embarrassed and totally exposed. Yolanda turned and saw me plainly. This was it. There was no coming back from this. We were sunk. This investigation was over. Arthur was never going to get justice.

But I underestimated my best friend. Tania had a plan, and she was about to spring into action. She stomped over to me, grabbed my arm, and hoisted me up to my feet forcefully.

"First you fire me and now you're stalking me!" Tania shouted.

"I don't know what you mean," I said.

"You know exactly what I mean!" she responded in an angry tone.

After that, she took the glass of water at my table and threw it in my face. Oh my, I was soaked, but Tania wasn't done. She slapped me. It wasn't hard, but she slapped me nonetheless. Was this going to turn into a fistfight? Really, she was going overboard now. She pulled me close and whispered in my ear what Tom told her.

Reggie now sprang into action himself. He rose to his feet as if he was going to break up the "fight." He pulled Tania close and whispered, "Good show. Your timing is amazing!"

After that, Tom and Yolanda came to our table.

"I take it back, Tom, I think I like this one. She might be a keeper," Yolanda said before she walked out of the restaurant. Tom and Tania followed behind her. Tom was quite the doting puppy when it came to Yolanda. What a scene, what a situation we caused, but it was worth it.

The host came over to see how I was. She apologized for the others. She even offered us a free lunch, which we took full advantage of. It was clear Tom was a regular and they wanted to keep his business and defuse the situation, so we didn't get angered by Tom's rude guest. Little did she know the rude guest was my best friend.

"That was great!" Reggie said. "She's amazing!"

"Yup, she is," I said. "Tania is a remarkable woman."

We sat back at our table and settled in. There I was with a wet blouse and tousled hair, but it was all worth it.

"We have somewhere to go, Reggie," I said.

"Where are we going?"

"We need to go to the police."

"Why would we do that?" Reggie questioned.

"Because Tania whispered to me what she found out. Yolanda is not one of Tom's clients, she's his only client. We need to go to the police and tell them what we know so they can look at Tom's financials linking him to Yolanda. I'm sure those books are going to be page-turners. We're going to get her."

CHAPTER 18
THE CAVALRY ISN'T COMING

Welcome back to the police station. My old home away from home. I remember the long hours I spent here as a reporter interviewing people waiting for trial, police officers, DAs, etc. I loved it. Of course, I was never totally fulfilled, but I always put my all in the stories I was given. As a reporter, you have to be determined and have pride of authorship; after all, it's your byline and your reputation. Along the way I met a lot of good people and made a few friendships. The only one I kept in touch with is Anthony. He was always a sweetheart. He listens to me. He takes me seriously. It's nice to have someone there that treats you like an equal. I especially needed that given my work environment at the time.

"Are you sure this is a good move?" Reggie questioned.

"Why not?" I asked.

"Our last visit here was not so successful," Reggie responded.

"This time, we have a theory," I said.

"We do, but we don't have much else," Reggie noted sarcastically.

"If I didn't know better, I would think you were putting cold water on this little visit," I countered forcefully.

"I'm just not sure your friend Lieutenant Crooks is going to help us, Dimples. He didn't help us before, so I don't think we are going to have a better outcome this time around. Maybe I'm wrong, but I don't think I am."

I wasn't going to let him stop me from telling the police. Crooks was going to listen. He was going to have no choice but to listen. As I looked ahead, I saw him look back at me. He tried to run around the corner of his office hallway, but I darted toward him and stopped him in his tracks. I tapped him on the shoulder, and he begrudgingly turned to face me.

"We don't have anything new to report, but if we did, I would not report it to you anyway, so I think you better just go," he said condescendingly.

"Actually, I have something to report to you."

"Here we go!" he shouted in disbelief. Did he think his little insult was going to deter me? Obviously, he did not know me as well as he thought.

"We know who killed Arthur. It was his mother, Yolanda," I said with confidence.

"Are you crazy?" Crooks responded in shock.

"We interviewed Yolanda's best friend and we found out Yolanda viewed Arthur as a meal ticket and not a son. Arthur was working up some kind of plan to benefit his family, but I don't think it was going well based on the calls I overheard the morning of his murder," I explained.

"You did what?" he asked in an angry tone. "You are not a crime reporter anymore. And don't think analyzing crime online through your little blog counts for anything because it doesn't. If I hear you are getting involved in a police investigation, there will be hell to pay! You need to leave!"

"I will not," I shot back. "We also learned that Yolanda and Tom, Arthur's friend, are full business partners in some real estate venture."

"Who cares?" Crooks asked. "She can be in business with whoever she wants. I don't care and neither should you. As far as I am concerned, this is still a mugging, and that's final unless new evidence comes to light, which it hasn't."

"Does that mean this matter is closed?" I asked.

"I've already said too much to you. You don't have any new

evidence, just some crazy ideas running around in that little head of yours. I better not hear that you are harassing people because I will come after you!" Crooks warned as he walked away.

"I told you this was going to be a big waste of time," Reggie said with an air of confidence.

"True gentlemen never say I told you so," I answered back.

Now what do we do? Where do we go from here? These thoughts were bouncing around in my head. Thankfully, Tania was still embedded with Tom. That gave me the warm fuzzies because we still had a chance of getting some hard evidence linking Tom with Yolanda that could possibly prove they hired those people to kill poor Arthur. We were not out of avenues to follow just yet, but I still wasn't giving up totally on the police.

Reggie was walking back toward the entrance when I spotted Anthony. I quickly stopped Reggie and motioned him to look at Anthony. Reggie had no idea what I was doing. He looked at me strangely and then placed his hand on my forehead as if to check if I had a fever.

"Are you okay? What are you doing?" he asked.

"It's my friend Anthony over there. I have to talk to him. He'll take me seriously," I said with conviction.

Anthony was talking to another officer next to the watercooler in the corner of the room. She was tall and skinny and typically beautiful, but then again, so was Anthony. What a man! As I was looking at Anthony, Reggie was looking at me with eyes filled with disdain.

"Wasn't he talking to another woman when we were here last?" Reggie asked.

"It's Anthony, he's always talking to a girl. Just look at him. Can you blame the ladies for wanting to chat it up with him?" I asked.

That comment obviously upset Reggie. He let out a gruff noise and walked away from me. He said he would wait for me in the car, and if I thought Anthony was going to help us, I was wrong. He was wrong. I knew Anthony would help us. Besides, I don't know what Reggie was so mad about; I was solving the murder with him and Tania, not Anthony. He didn't even know Anthony, so what was his problem?

Who cares. I knew Anthony and that's what matters. So I walked over to Anthony, who was still talking with that blonde.

I tried to wiggle my way into the conversation, but the blonde wouldn't have it. She just kept on talking. She knew I was there, and she just ignored me. Well, that was not going to do; that was not going to do at all. I would not be ignored. After what seemed like forever just waiting there, I decided to speak up and asked her when the last time was she dyed her hair because it was obviously dark brown. That little comment got her attention because she finally turned to address me. She told me last week and walked away, leaving Anthony all to me.

"That wasn't very nice, Sheila," Anthony scolded.

"She wasn't very nice. Anyway, I need your help," I said, almost begging.

"You know I can't resist you. What's up?" Anthony asked.

"We got some info indicating that Yolanda was not the ideal mother. In fact, she is a business partner with Arthur's friend. There's got to be a connection," I explained.

"You know it's not wise for you to be involved in this investigation. Everyone is convinced it is just a mugging gone very wrong. In fact, Clarence wants this whole thing to go away so it does not complicate his election. He doesn't want race relations to dominate this town," Anthony reported.

"I know, but what can I do?" I replied. "And if everyone here thinks it is a mugging, they won't be looking any further into any of it and nothing will happen. This case will never be solved. I can't stand by and let that happen. You know me!"

"I know, but promise you'll keep me informed," Anthony said forcefully. "Don't go to Crooks, just come straight to me and I'll help any way I can. I have your back and I'll help if I can, just let me know what you're up to."

"I promise to keep you in the loop," I said. He kissed me on the forehead and walked away. As he did that, the blonde gave me the dirtiest look. It wasn't a romantic kiss; it was more like a kiss a brother would give his sister. I think that's what it was anyway.

Just as I thought I was done at the police station, another advocate approached me; this time it was DA Clarence Wright. He seemed determined to talk to me.

"I heard you had it out with Crooks again," Clarence said.

"It's nothing new," I replied. Crooks just hates me. He always hated me. He's just holier than thou. He thinks he's God or something. Crooks is one of those police officers that thinks only he can solve every crime and civilians like me are just a waste of time. Well, I am not a waste of time! I was going to show him. I was going to solve this crime and reveal to the world it was nothing short of a murder.

"Don't let him bother you," Clarence said with a tender voice. "You know how he is."

"I know, but he gets to me," I confessed. "He rubs me the wrong way."

"He tells me you still think Arthur whoever was murdered," Clarence noted. "Do you really think so? Everyone is saying he was mugged."

"I know, but that's not what I saw. I saw a murder," I reported with conviction. I was determined to at least convince Clarence. After a second, I calmed down. He'd recently lost his father and he was running for governor, so I knew he couldn't deal with this right now. "I'm sorry. I don't mean to bother you about this. I know you're busy and you don't want a murder circling around you with this election. Also, I know you recently lost your father; it must be very hard."

"It is, Sheila," Clarence confided. "My father was such a hero to me. I wish he were here. I have so many questions for him."

"I envy you," I admitted. "My father left when I was young and it was just me, my mom, and my younger brother. It would have been nice to have a father to look up to."

"Fathers are people too. They make mistakes. They fall short, but they are still your dad," Clarence said with a smile. I could see his eyes watering a bit. Poor Clarence. I could see the sorrow and the pain on his face. He was really hurting; this was not a cheap political act designed to score points, it was an honest moment whereby a son was grieving the loss of his father. "It's the family unit that will get you through anything and everything. You can't break that unit, no matter what you do. That's what my political campaign is about. That's what I'm about. I have to be true to that."

"I know you do," I said. "I won't bother you guys again about this."

"That's good," he replied. He was very relieved. He put both of his hands on my shoulders. "What you saw was horrible, but I'm sure it was a mugging. What else could it have been? There is no other explanation, really. It has to be a simple mugging."

"I guess you're right," I said to make him feel better.

"You call me if you need anything," he said as he turned and walked away.

I had to lie to him. What else was I going to do? He had too much on his plate as it was. Besides, he was a typical politician, so he couldn't really be relied upon. Clarence was so wrapped up in appearances he couldn't be objective. Maybe it was a genetic defect all politicians got at birth, but they all seemed to be mainly concerned with themselves, in my humble opinion. Clarence was nice, but that gene didn't skip him. He was a politician through and through.

Going to the police was a mistake. We got nowhere, but I was not going to admit that to Reggie when I got back in the car. He was quick to ask about Anthony. I told him Anthony would help, but we would have to do all the investigating. Reggie just laughed. He just didn't like Anthony. I tried to cheer myself up by calling Tania, but she didn't pick up. She was busy with Tom, and I was going to have to wait for her to call me. I knew that, but waiting was not something I enjoyed doing. I guess I would have to get used to it. Let's face it, the cavalry isn't coming. We were going to have to solve this murder on our own, and that's exactly what we were going to do.

CHAPTER 19
EXPOSED

We went back to my house. Time to get to work, real work. I have to write my column and go through my email to see if all the contributed content has come in. From there, my new copy editor, Reggie, has to read through everything before we post it to our website and social media. To the average person, it might seem very boring, but I think it's exciting.

As Reggie and I stepped into the house together, we were greeted by Majesta. She brushed up to my leg lovingly. I could tell she was excited to see me.

"He's back again?" Majesta asked lovingly.

I looked down at her and shushed her.

"It's okay, I like him," she said before jumping on the sofa to stretch out.

Majesta is a good judge of character, and I agree with her; I like Reggie too. However, that was enough of that; we had work to do. So Reggie and I settled in and I started going through my email and passing him stories to edit for today's edition. I had to admit it has been nice to have Reggie around; usually it's just me and Tania.

"So how was your chat with Anthony?" Reggie asked curtly.

"Fine," I responded, equally as curtly. I was not going to let

Reggie's apparent hard feelings toward my friend Anthony get me down.

"He's not going to help, is he?" Reggie asked as if he knew the answer.

"He can't investigate anything because there's a lot of pressure to just call it a mugging and be done with it, but if we need him, he will help. He said I should avoid Crooks and just come to him directly," I said.

"I'll bet he did, Dimples," Reggie replied sarcastically.

I wasn't going to engage. Obviously, Reggie was not a fan of Anthony, and I wasn't going to convince him otherwise; it was a lost cause. Besides, Reggie was helping me out here, so why should I risk upsetting him over something so trivial? It was best to just keep working and wait to see if Tania found out anything of interest. Tom was up to something with Yolanda, and I was convinced it had something to do with Arthur.

"I can't thank you enough for filling in for Tania," I said to Reggie. I didn't want to see him mad. He was much more fun to be around when he was focused on something he enjoys; I guess we all are. Who wants to think about something that brings forth feelings of anger? Nobody, that's who.

"No problem at all. These articles are all really well-written and quite a lot of fun to read," Reggie replied pleasantly. I could see his mood was improving. *Now that's the Reggie I love*—I mean, love to be around.

Then, my cell phone rang. It was Tania! Yup, I knew she would report in soon. Tania had another plan, and it was a good one.

"What's going on?" Reggie asked.

"Yolanda and Tom were not too happy about our lunch. Yolanda came to the office in a huff. She wants an offsite meeting with Tom. She invited him to her house."

"What does that have to do with us?" Reggie asked.

"Well, while Tom is out of the office, Tania thinks we should snoop around. We'll look around the office, and she'll stay at her post at the front desk to keep a lookout. She doesn't want to risk him seeing her going through his office, so she thinks we should do it while she acts as our lookout," I explained.

"Sounds good to me. Let's go, my dear lady, your chariot awaits," Reggie said, motioning to the front door. Great! Reggie was back, in true theatrical form.

We got to Tom's office real quick. Reggie was in a hurry, and I appreciated that. Once we got to Tom's office, I gave Tania a big hug. She looked down at my blouse and she could see the water stain still there from when she threw that glass of water on me. I should have changed once we got back to my house, but I didn't think to. My mind was full of work stuff—and Arthur's demise, of course. Clothing details sometimes escape me. I am always so focused on the task in front of me at the time that I don't pay much attention to my appearance. I know it's a failing, but that's me. I pay closer attention to every source in a story than I do if my shoe color matches my blouse color. What can I say? I'm not a fashionista.

"I'm so sorry about the water," Tania said remorsefully.

"Don't worry about it."

"And I'm sorry about that slap too. Good thing you don't have a black eye or something, though," Tania said, as if to excuse her earlier behavior.

"Don't worry about it," I said again.

"What do you mean?" Reggie piped in. "That was perfect! You were great! Your improvisation skills are off the charts!" Reggie was obviously impressed by Tania's little show, but he wasn't the one that got slapped and wet. No matter now. It was a good move, and Tom and Yolanda were obviously convinced or Tom wouldn't have left Tania alone in his office. Tania was a good actress, something Reggie valued.

Beyond her acting abilities, Tania was always a good friend. Ever since college, Tania and I have been inseparable. She's like the sister I never had. Don't get me wrong, I love my brother, Johnnie, and he means well, but he's always chasing the next "big thing." It was nice to have someone in my corner who was a bit impulsive but also very grounded in helping me. Tania always had my best interests at heart.

"Well, let's get to work," I ordered. "Tania, you stay at your desk and make sure Tom doesn't come back. Reggie and I will look through his office."

It was a great plan. What could go wrong? Reggie and I ran into Tom's office and started looking around. It was a very neat office. I guess it was neat because he apparently didn't have much to do, which was good for us because that meant we had less to look through.

Reggie quickly found some paperwork on Tom's desk that caught his eye. It looked like a proposal of some kind.

"Check this out," Reggie said. "They are looking to sell a building. It's an office building in town. I know that building. That's where the Wal-Mart is. Remember that?"

"How could I forget? We almost got arrested," I laughed.

"It was a good time," Reggie responded. We both laughed at that point. "Look, here's another document where they are talking about selling an apartment building in town, and here's another one about selling a local hotel. Someone is looking to go liquid. As they say, cash is king, I guess."

"Why would they want to sell those buildings? They're all so profitable, I assume." I motioned for Reggie to give me those documents. As I was skimming through them, I noticed a commonality that was surely evidence. "Notice anything else about these documents?"

Reggie took them back and looked them over. "No. What do you see?"

"The owner of all three buildings is Yolanda." How could she own all three of those buildings? She did not appear to be that rich and if she was, why would she be angry at Arthur for coming up with some plan he was convinced would bring in more money? It didn't make sense. Maybe I misinterpreted the call.

"Wait a minute," Reggie said with alarm in his voice.

"What's the matter?"

"Tania said Tom went to an offsite meeting with Yolanda, and we find all these documents on his desk about buildings Yolanda owns," Reggie noted.

"So what?"

"This must be what they are meeting about, Dimples, and he left the documents here at his office, which means he'll be back once he notices he left them behind."

We turned around, facing the door to his office, and there was Tom with Tania on his arm. We looked at Tania and she shrugged back at us. We were caught—all three of us were caught. Now I know what cat burglars feel like when they're nabbed by the police with the stolen goods in their possession.

"I tried to stop him from coming in, but he rushed past me," Tania said.

"What is going on here?" Tom asked. He was fuming. I have never seen someone look so heated before. "How did you two get in here, and why are you going through my things?"

"I know this looks bad—" I started.

"Yes, it does!" Tom yelled back at me.

"When we were here last, Sheila lost an earring," Reggie said in a hurried tone.

"What?" Tom responded incredulously.

"Sheila lost one of her earrings, and she thinks the last place she felt it on her ear was in your office. So we came back to look for it. We didn't think to call ahead and when we got here you were out, so Tania said we could look for it," Reggie explained.

It was a great story! I guess Tania wasn't the only member of this team that could think on their feet. I was so lucky to have Reggie and Tania on my side, but I have to admit, I am getting a little jealous that the two of them keep finding ways to get us out of these jams and I am at a loss. I'm supposed to be the star reporter here. I guess I'm only good at asking the questions, which, in thinking about it further, is a good quality, to be sure. I probably shouldn't beat myself up so much and just be grateful for all the assists.

"Yup, it's the diamond ones she got for her birthday last year from her mother," Tania said.

"I don't know what's going on here, but it's not right. It's just not right," Tom noted. "Ever since I met you three, things have gone upside down. I was very happy running my business. You just don't seem to go away, for some reason."

"We are so sorry," I said. "We'll go right now. We won't bother you again, I promise."

We were in the clear. We got out of this situation with no harm done. Reggie and I started walking toward the door, but Tom stopped us.

"No, there's something strange with you three," Tom said. "I can't chance it anymore. You and you are going." He pointed at me and Reggie. "But you are going too." He pointed at Tania.

"Me?" Tania asked. "Why me? I need this job."

"Quite frankly, I don't care," Tom replied with authority. "I can't jeopardize what I have going on here, and in one day I witnessed a catfight and two people rifling through my office. I can't explain it, but I know it's all wrong. Tania, you are fired!"

"No, you can't!" Tania yelled.

"I've had enough. All three of you have to go," Tom commanded.

Tania got her things and the three of us left the office. Tania's time undercover was terminated. We gave it our best effort, but it didn't work out. Let's face it, the three of us were not built to be private investigators; we were all writers.

"Now what?" Tania asked. She wasn't going to give up, and neither was Reggie.

"Yeah, what's our next move?" Reggie asked. He wasn't going to abandon this effort to find out what really happened to Arthur either. After all, it meant a lot to him, being a Black man and just a decent human being.

"I don't know, I just don't know," I said, defeated.

Tania and Reggie both stared at me. I guess they couldn't believe I said that. Given everything that had happened up until now, I guess I couldn't blame them. I had been the one driving this investigation. It was all I could talk about. All I could think about. Let's face it, I was obsessed. Solving Arthur's murder had been an obsession, and obsessions are just not healthy.

"What can we do? We've been exposed. I don't think we have any other leads to follow," I said ruefully. "I guess it's over."

CHAPTER 20
I KNEW IT ALL ALONG

W e'd been caught, and not even Tania could talk her way out of things totally. I remember when Tania and I were in college together just like yesterday. We didn't have many of the same classes, but we did have freshman English together. It was a great class. The professor was amazing. She inspired me to be a writer. Tania, on the other hand, just wanted to pass the class. What can I say? That's Tania for you.

Anyway, this new guy came in the class after the second week. I think his name was Jake or Justin; who can remember these things? Anyway, let's just say his name was Jake. He was shy and reserved, and Tania liked him. Tania liked him a lot, in fact.

One afternoon, Jake was in the same lunch line as Tania and me. He was a sporty guy, so he had some fruit, a bottle of water, and some cereal, I think. Tania and I were loaded down with soda, chips, and pizza. College is not a time to watch your weight, at least it wasn't for Tania and me.

Jake was now paying for his food. The Bear was his teller. We called her The Bear because she was tall and stocky and all-around big. Everyone hated her. She was gruff and rude to the students. People like that are missing something in their lives, so they take those frustrations out on others. You know the kind of person I'm talking about, don't you?

Jake's card wasn't working, so The Bear insisted he pay with cash or he would have to put his food back. It was quite an embarrassing situation for poor Jake to find himself in. Tania quickly sprang into action to help him. She told The Bear Jake had the cash in his back pocket, if she would just give him a second. Tania slipped a twenty-dollar bill into his back pocket and pinched his butt in the process. Jake jumped a bit, feeling Tania's hand on his butt; however, he needed the assist, so he gave The Bear the money Tania slipped him. That's Tania for you. She's always there to help, and she always has a plan. Too bad the money drop didn't quite do the trick. Tania asked Jake out, but he declined.

That's just how things were going now. Tania tried to get us out of hot water with Tom, and she did, but he still kicked all three of us to the curb. Our undercover plan was a big bust and we were at a loss. So we regrouped back at my house to discuss our next steps.

"You guys are back so soon," my calico, Majesta, said to me as she greeted me at the door. "I guess things didn't go so well. By the way, can I get a treat?"

I went to the kitchen to get the treat before joining Tania and Reggie in the living room. Sure, I owned my own online publishing company, but Majesta was the true boss. No matter, she was a cutie. I'm just like those stereotypical parents whose kids have them wrapped around their fingers, listening to their every request.

"What's our next move?" Reggie asked.

"I don't know," I responded glumly.

"We keep going. We are getting closer, I know it," Tania said enthusiastically.

"Maybe we should start one of those murder boards to document what we know," I suggested. I have a great memory so unlike most reporters, I rarely kept a notebook.

"You watch too much TV," Tania noted. "We don't need a murder board; we need an idea and a plan to get more on Yolanda. She's still our prime suspect. She must have hired the killers. We know she has money. Look at all the properties she owns!"

"Tania's right," I pointed out. "She does seem to have money, and Tom is her partner, helping her invest it and manage it. But if she is well off, why was Arthur so determined to embark on some big-money scheme that obviously got him killed?"

"You know what? Money doesn't grow on trees," Tania answered. "Maybe the money was about to dry up; that's why Yolanda is selling the properties."

That was true. We saw those documents in Tom's office trying to sell those three properties. Every good detective always says to follow the money and you'll find your motive and your killer, but I wasn't convinced. This was a family affair, and sometimes those things can get tricky when you add emotion into your business dealings. Things can get real messy, real fast.

Reggie just sat there listening intently to me and Tania as we went back and forth, talking through what we know and what we suspect. I could tell he was deep in thought. I could see the wheels spinning in his head.

"I have an idea," he chimed in. "Let's just ask her."

"What do you mean?" I responded, confused.

"All roads still point to Yolanda, so let's just go to her house and confront her with what we know," Reggie said.

"Yes!" Tania cried in affirmation of Reggie's plan. The two of them quickly got up and got back in their jackets. They were ready to go see Yolanda straight away.

I just sat on the sofa for a second in thought. Was this the best way forward? What would happen if we were wrong? I thought about it for a second, and then I got up and followed them. What do we have to lose? I thought; let's give it a try. In no time, we climbed in the car and were off to confront Yolanda.

It was easy to track down Yolanda's house. Her name was listed, and we got the address quite easily. As we pulled up to her house, it was very noticeable she was well off. Her lawn was well-groomed, and she had colorful bushes lining her house, which looked newly painted tan. Also, she had a red Porsche parked in her driveway. This was a woman that was comfortable.

Tania agreed to wait in the car while Reggie and I went in. She didn't want to be seen with us, just in case we needed her to cozy up to Yolanda later on. With our avenues of discovery closing, we had to keep as much open as possible if this did not go well. My guess was that Yolanda wouldn't confess, but maybe we could catch her off guard. Lies are like mosquitos; they'll find you wherever you are and suck you dry. Once you get caught in a lie, you're done for.

We rang the doorbell and Yolanda promptly answered. She was not at all surprised to see us. I swear, every time I saw this woman, her stoicism just struck me. Does she get upset about anything? You can't get an ounce of feeling out of her. It's like she's robotic or something.

"It took you long enough to arrive," Yolanda said with a smirk. "I've been expecting you."

Reggie looked just as stunned as I did. It's hard to believe a mother could kill her child or in any way be responsible for the death of her child, but if there's any mother out there that could do such a horrendous act, it was Yolanda. We followed behind her without saying a word as she led us through her house. We were taken to a grand living room with dark-leather sofas, glass side tables, and a grand crystal chandelier hanging from the ceiling. As I said earlier, this woman was comfortable.

"Please, have a seat," she said. "I heard you were snooping in Tom's office. Did you find anything interesting?"

Again, her conversation took me for a loop, but it was time to dig in and see what was really going on here. "As a matter of fact, we did," I responded. "We saw that you own at least three properties in town, and you're looking to sell them. We also discovered that you and Tom are partners."

"You are correct," she said, emotionless. "I actually own several properties. I introduced Arthur and Shanice to Tom, and they became fast friends. Tom helps me manage my finances and my properties."

"So what was Arthur up to that you needed him stopped?" I asked.

"What are you talking about?" Yolanda asked coyly.

"I heard your conversation with Arthur just before he died. He was working on something you did not approve of," I replied forcefully.

"A mother doesn't always have to approve of what her children are up to, does she?" Yolanda noted coldly.

"We also talked to your friend Eugenia. She told us you had little to no relationship with Arthur, and she told us why you named him Arthur," Reggie interrupted.

It was all true, of course, but I wasn't sure we should put all of our cards on the table so soon. Any normal person might have thrown us out after that comment, but Yolanda just listened politely. This was obviously no normal person.

"Eugenia is a sweetheart, isn't she?" Yolanda mentioned. "She helped me a lot with Arthur. I think she saw him as a son. She was probably projecting. The poor dear never married, so she has no children of her own."

"Don't you get it? I saw your son murdered!" I blurted. I just couldn't hold back. "Two police officers beat him to death in an alley. Well, we thought they were police officers, but none of the police officers in town fit the description, so we assume they were hired guns."

"That's a very interesting story. The police told me it was a mugging, and until evidence comes up proving otherwise, I think I'll trust the police," Yolanda pointed out.

"You hired those people to keep your son from doing whatever he was about to do," I accused.

"I was told by the police you're a pest and I should ignore you. I think I've put up with enough. I did not kill my son. My son was mugged in an alley. He was in the wrong place at the wrong time. Now, unless you have anything substantive to say to me, I think you should leave," Yolanda said as she stood up as if to escort us out.

"One more tiny question," I said. "What kind of mother doesn't cry when mourning the death of her son?"

"A mother determined to survive," Yolanda responded coldly.

My phone rang and I asked to go to the powder room. It was just Tania calling to see if we were getting anywhere. Unfortunately, we were not. Yolanda led us out of the house. Just as she turned to walk away, I ran around the corner of the house. Tania wasn't the only woman of action around here. As I was running around the back of the house, I tripped on a garden hose, but I wasn't going to let that stop me.

It was a bright, hot, sunny day, so the sliding door in the back of the house that opened to a deck was wide open. I noticed it was open when we were in the house. I could see Yolanda sitting on the sofa inside the house. She was on the phone. I heard her say she just had to leave for a little while and she asked the caller to help her. It worked after all. We rattled her, and now she must be going on the run.

Reggie snuck up behind me and asked, "What is she doing?"

"She's planning her getaway," I responded. "Let's go back to the car and wait this out. She was just on the phone asking for someone to help her get away. Maybe that person is on the way here."

Once we got back in the car with Tania, we saw Yolanda putting a few small bags in her car. She was obviously planning for a little excursion somewhere. This was the break we needed, to see where she went and what she would do next.

Then, the unexpected happened. A Jeep pulled up to her house and a man got out carrying a large envelope. I didn't see his face, but I remembered that brown hair and big, brown beard. That was the man I saw on top of Arthur—it had to be.

He kissed Yolanda's hand after she greeted him at the door. After that, he gave her an envelope and left. I was stunned. She was having an affair with the man that killed her son? Reggie insisted it looked like a polite kiss and not a romantic one, but still. That was the murderer, and Yolanda knew him. In fact, not only did she know him, but he gave her some kind of envelope.

"What do we do now?" Reggie asked.

"Yeah, what's our next move?" Tania questioned.

I had to think this through. We had to be deliberate. We had to be just as calculating as Yolanda was. But there was no time for that, as it turned out. Everything was happening so fast. She was leaving the house and getting in her car. We were too late to be proactive; we had to be reactive, and not let her out of our sight. Murderers get sloppy when they feel cornered. This was our moment to really figure out once and for all what was going on. Yolanda knew a lot more than she told us, and we were going to find out the whole story.

"You're too quiet, Sheila. What are you thinking?" Tania asked. She always knew when I was lost in thought. She knew me too well.

I knew exactly what to do. All my years as a reporter told me to follow my leads and keep following them until they went cold.

I said, "I knew it. She has to be behind this murder. I say we follow her and solve this murder right here and now."

CHAPTER 21
THE GREAT ESCAPE

Now we were finally getting somewhere. That man was the man I saw beating Arthur. Why would he be giving Yolanda an envelope if she didn't know him? And why would he be kissing her hand once he saw her? She's guilty! She hired those people to kill her own son to stop him from doing whatever he was doing, I just knew it. What other explanation was there?

Yolanda drove faster than Eugenia, so there was actual work for Reggie to do in order to keep up with her. It wasn't just a walk in the park this time, but it still wasn't a high-speed car chase either. Tania was getting a kick out of following Yolanda. She was definitely enjoying the ride.

"You're doing great, Reggie!" Tania said with encouragement.

"Thanks. I think we're going to get her this time," Reggie replied.

"And kudos to you too, Sheila, for coming up with the plan to spy on her and follow her. I'm usually the one coming up with these things," Tania said.

"I can be a woman of action too, you know," I said. "Now I'm going to call Anthony to tell him what's going on."

Reggie became defensive. He got very tense. "Why do we need to call him again? We don't even know where Yolanda is going," Reggie noted.

"True, but my guess is she is headed for the train station or the airport, and she just passed the intersection for the train station, so my guess is she's headed for the airport," I replied.

I got out my cell phone and called Anthony. He responded quickly and said he would meet us at the airport. I knew he wouldn't let me down.

"Good news, Anthony is going to meet us at the airport," I said to everyone.

"Of course he is," Reggie said sarcastically.

I wasn't sure what Reggie had against Anthony, but we needed the police involved. We couldn't do this alone. After all, we were amateurs. They're the pros. If someone needed help writing a great newspaper article, I think they would call me instead of some guy that knows nothing about journalism. I've never been a person that's afraid to ask for help. In the end, you only know what you know, so you figure out the rest with a little help if you can get it, or on your own if you can't. Either way, you can't let yourself be shaken off of accomplishing your goal. Achieving your goal is the North Star, in that you have to follow it in order to get to where you're destined to be.

"I just don't know what Anthony brings to the table," Reggie said.

"He has a badge," I replied.

"Who cares? I have a badge too. It's in the back seat somewhere among all those costumes," Reggie noted.

Tania laughed as she looked through the items in the back seat next to her. After tossing things about, she found the fake police badge. "He isn't kidding, there actually is a badge back here," she said, laughing.

"Laugh if you want, but those costumes come in handy," Reggie said, offended.

I started laughing too. I wasn't laughing at Reggie, I was laughing because I was happy. Who but me has two friends that would help her on this crazy journey to track down a killer? And Reggie is a new friend. He literally just moved in next door, and here he was acting as my wingman throughout this whole thing. *I'm a lucky lady; a lucky lady indeed.*

Just as I suspected, Yolanda was pulling into the airport. She was parking her car in the extended stay parking lot and gathering her bags. She couldn't get away from us this easily. Does she know who she is dealing with? Well, she doesn't know us, so I guess not, but she soon would. We were not giving up on Arthur.

"I think she's getting out of her car," Tania said. "You two should follow her. I'll wait here for Anthony." Tania winked at me. She obviously thought it was a good idea for me and Reggie to continue our little partnership in shaking down Yolanda.

"I guess that sounds okay," I responded with a smile. It was a good idea. I enjoyed being around Reggie, but I wasn't sure if the feeling was mutual; at least not as mutual as it was for me.

"That sounds like a plan to me too," Reggie said with an air of determination, but before we left the car, he motioned to Tania in the back seat. "Give me that badge; we may need it."

Yolanda was headed to the airport's main doors in a hurry. She obviously wanted to get on a plane. I wondered where she was headed, probably to some faraway island. She would be on a beach sipping cold alcoholic drinks while her son was buried in the ground.

In moments like this, I reflected on my upbringing and my mother. When my father disappeared, things were horrible, but my mother kept it together; she made sure me and my brother were taken care of. I'm not a mother, but I hope if I am one day, I'll be like my mother, and not the shell of a mother we were following now. This woman was a mother in the biological sense, but not in the real sense. She named her son after a fairy tale because she thought she could get something out of being Arthur's mother, and when that advantage went away, she discarded him; discarded him in the worst sense.

We saw her at the counter now, getting her ticket. She was an older woman, so using the kiosk wasn't an option for her, apparently. She needed to wait in line and speak to a real person, and that worked to our advantage because it gave us more time to get close to her, but not enough time. We live in an increasingly technological world, so the line to speak to a real person and not a machine was short. She zipped through, got her ticket, and was off to security.

We followed behind. We had to confront her about how she knew that man; the man that kissed her hand; the man that handed her an envelope; the man that killed her son. As we arrived at security, she was far ahead, and I started to panic a bit.

"What are we going to do?" I asked in a sweat.

"She won't get away from us," Reggie promised.

"She's too far ahead of us. We will never get to that point in the line this way," I noted. I must have sounded totally defeated because Reggie looked at me and grabbed my hand tight at the same time. He was not going to let me give up at this moment. Reggie was confident in his will. He knew what he wanted, and he was going to go for it, all the way. He was not just going to dip his little toe in the water; he was jumping in headfirst.

"I need to get ahead!" Reggie yelled. "I need to get by!"

Everyone's head turned. They were shocked. They were all thinking to themselves, what is going on here? My guess is there was a bit of fear as well. We live in a scary world, and when someone starts yelling in an airport, it's alarming. It's a shame that's where we are, but that's the reality.

Now Reggie had everyone's attention, but what was he going to do with it? "I'm a police officer, and I need to get to the front of the line!" Once those words came out of his mouth, everyone seemed to calm down a bit and the people in the line stepped aside. Everyone let Reggie by, and I followed behind him. Thankfully, nobody looked too hard at the badge Reggie was brandishing.

We were getting closer and closer to Yolanda. She was just about to walk into the body scanner to detect if she had any shady objects on her person. Too bad that machine can't scan into a person's soul because if it could, it would surely detect something horrible.

Yolanda turned around and she now saw us progressing toward her. This is the point in the television episode where the criminal makes a run for it and is tackled to the floor by the valiant hero, but that's not what happened here. In true Yolanda form, she did not run. She stood very still and stared straight at the two of us. It was a bit scary, to be honest. She seemed so cold and removed from the gravity of the situation she was in. Yolanda just was not fazed at all.

"This man is not a police officer," she said.

One of the security guards came up to us and looked at Reggie's badge. He quickly grabbed it out of Reggie's hand. We were caught again. Just like that, Yolanda got the better of us. She bested us at every turn. We were outmaneuvered.

The security guard knew the badge was a fake and asked us to come with him. We couldn't avoid it this time, we were going to go to jail. Impersonating a police officer is a crime.

Just as we turned toward the guard, ready to walk away from Yolanda, Anthony and Tania appeared behind us.

"That may not be a real badge, but this is," Anthony said.

"Yes, it is!" said Tania, encouraging Anthony.

"I would like to hear what the lady has to say," Anthony continued.

Reggie said something under his breath I could not hear, but regardless, now was my moment to solve this crime. I just had to use all my skill and ask all the right questions. Yolanda may have been a world-class schemer, but she wasn't a world-class journalist. Journalists ask questions with ease and we get to the truth.

"Where are you going, exactly?" I asked.

"On a vacation," Yolanda said. "Is that a crime?"

"I'll decide what's a crime and what's not," Anthony said.

"Yeah, that's right!" Tania yelled.

Yolanda was cornered and she knew it. She was going to have to work harder to get out of this one. She was going to have to call on all her wits to outsmart me.

"I heard you on the phone telling someone you had to leave and you needed his help. Why?" I asked.

"My only child has died, and ever since that happened, you and your friends have been stalking me. I need a vacation," she answered with an air of superiority about her.

"We're not stalking you; we are trying to figure out who killed your son," I said in response.

"You're crazy. The police say my son was mugged; why isn't that good enough for you?" Yolanda asked.

"It's not good enough because I saw your son die, and it was not a mugging. I saw it with my own eyes, and I may be many things, but I am not blind," I responded with force. "After making that call I overheard you make earlier, a man came to your door with an envelope. What was in the envelope?"

"Here it is. Look for yourself," Yolanda said as she tossed the envelope toward me. I knelt down to pick it up. I looked inside to find the plane ticket and some money. "Are you satisfied? Can I go now?" she asked harshly.

"What kind of a person delivers a plane ticket and some cash when called upon?" I asked.

"I have many friends. I have many male friends, that is. If I need a break, I call a friend and I get help; that's how I work. That's how I've always worked. It pays to have powerful friends you know will have your back," Yolanda shared.

"I don't have those types of friends and, by the way, what did you do to get those types of friends, exactly?" I asked.

"I think this has gone on long enough," Anthony said. "It doesn't seem like there's anything concrete here, Sheila. Are you going somewhere with your questions?"

"My question exactly," Yolanda said confidently.

"The man that gave you the envelope is the man that killed your son. I'm sure of it. And I just saw him kiss your hand and give you this envelope. Explain that."

Yolanda looked genuinely stunned. Her eyes widened. I don't think she was expecting that question, but she got it, nonetheless. Now she had to answer for her sins, for setting up the murder of her own son. The big reveal was finally here. She had to confess.

"I don't know the man that gave me the envelope. I've never met him before. I called someone else, and I guess he sent that man to give me the envelope. Now can I go?" Yolanda asked Anthony.

"I think so," he answered.

Yolanda walked away, but she turned back around to face us. She had something to say. "I'm not the type of woman to kiss and tell. Maybe if I were, you would get more answers. I need to rest. I'll be back in touch, though."

Yolanda walked away. As she was leaving for her gate, I shouted at her, "This is not over!"

Yolanda had escaped for now, but until the murder of her son was solved, she was not through with me, and I certainly was not through with her.

CHAPTER 22
COUPLING GONE WRONG

Things were not going well. Yolanda was our prime suspect and she got away. Also, our big investigation into Tom was a bust. We lost our inside hook when Tania got fired and we were exposed for snooping. This whole investigation had gone to hell.

As a little girl, I always wanted a pony. I dreamed and dreamed of riding that pony, with my hair flowing in the wind and my heart at ease. Me and my pony were going to be best friends. Obviously, I never got a pony. My mom had to work several jobs just to feed me and my brother, but I never stopped dreaming. That's who I am. I am a dreamer. I am a striver. I don't give up.

In the end, maybe I didn't get my pony, but I have my cat, Majesta; that counts for something. Also, I live on a great block with a lot of great neighbors, which is where I was headed. It was another neighbors dinner night. Dawn was supposed to host, but she asked if someone else could take their turn, and Sam and Ebony volunteered, so we were all going back to their house again. You would think after the big engagement acceptance between Alyssa and Dawn, this would be a great time to welcome the neighbors, but I guess not. Hosting can be stressful. I guess Dawn and Alyssa were just not up to it this time around.

Reggie and I arrived early to help Sam and Ebony out. We walked in on a bit of a family squabble. Their daughter, Jamie, was arguing with her parents. She was a freshman in high school, and she wanted to go out with her friends. Jamie was very popular at school. She had a lot of friends. Sam and Ebony resisted her entreaties to get out of the house, and she was having none of it.

The storm was brewing in that house tonight, and, boy, it was a violent one. There were phrases like: "I hate you!" swooshing through the air. Everything ended with a bunch of slammed doors. I guess that represented a clearing of all the activity because everything settled down after that. The house was quiet and calm again.

Their son was two years younger than Jamie. He was the exact opposite of his sister. He was quiet and reserved. He never caused any problems for his parents. I guess all the problems came leading up to his birth, so now he was making up for it. Ebony had a very tough birth. They thought they were going to lose him, but it was not to be. He was a little miracle. Sam and Ebony named him Ray because they saw his birth as a ray of light coming into their lives.

"Sorry for all the commotion," Ebony said.

"No worries at all," I responded. I could see that Ebony was very embarrassed, but these things happen. Teenagers will be teenagers, after all.

"Are you all settled into the house by now, Reggie?" Sam asked. He wanted to change the topic. He could see that his wife wanted to move on from the episode with Jamie as quickly as possible.

"Yup, it's great. I really love the house and the neighborhood," Reggie said.

"Now that you're a member of the club, you have to come and play ball with me and Ray," Tom said. "Ray's very reserved. I'm trying to get him into sports. Maybe it will bring him out of his shell a bit."

"I would love that. I'm really good with kids. I really want to be a dad someday," Reggie said with a huge smile on his face.

The smile on Ebony's face was just as huge. After Reggie proclaimed his fatherly impulses, she nudged me with her arm. I knew exactly what she was getting at. Reggie was pretty perfect in my mind, but I just wasn't sure he saw me that way. Oh well, I wasn't going to act like a teenage schoolgirl myself about it, I just had to keep moving forward.

The four of us got to talking, and Sam and Ebony were equally surprised Dawn and Alyssa passed on hosting tonight. I thought about it a bit further and I don't remember seeing much of either of them around after the proposal. No matter, I'm sure they were busy planning. It would be great to go to a wedding.

Sasha and Kamal showed up next, with Mother Millie in tow. After that, our resident Broadway diva, Olivia, entered in all her glory. We all greeted each other. These dinners were so amazing. We all really connected as neighbors and friends.

Time passed, and still Dawn and Alyssa were not there. Everyone was getting a little worried, but none of us said it out loud. We all had too much to talk about. As usual, Olivia was pumping Reggie for the latest theater news. Kamal and Sam were talking about baseball. Sasha and Millie were discussing recipes. Every corner of the house was filled with interesting conversation.

That's when Dawn and Alyssa arrived. The storm that passed earlier was coming around again. You could see it on their faces. They were both visibly angry. Something was not right. The newly engaged couple was clearly in turmoil.

"Sorry we're late," said Alyssa.

"She's been apologizing a lot lately," Dawn said sarcastically.

That comment was very telling. We all looked at each other. We were going to try and cut this storm off before it overtook all of us. Who wants to be stuck in bad weather? The answer is, nobody.

We gathered around the table to eat. Maybe good food would lighten the mood and welcome in the sunshine around here. After the first bite, Dawn snapped. She just couldn't hold it in.

"Alyssa here has not come out to her family and doesn't know if she ever will," Dawn said.

"It's not so easy for everyone. My family is not understanding like your family," Alyssa responded.

"So are we going to get married in secret? What will we tell your family as we celebrate our first anniversary? I know, we'll continue to say we're roomies," Dawn declared.

As the eldest of the bunch, Millie stepped in. "Times are hard. I know. I've been through hard times, but things get better."

"I just don't see how that's possible, Millie," Dawn replied.

"Look, child, we marched, we protested, we screamed and we shouted for everything we got nowadays, and even that seems like not much at times. They tried to stop us. They slapped us. They beat us. They turned their dogs on us. They turned water hoses on us. They used their batons. None of it worked. We overcame, and so will you," Millie advised the young couple.

"How did you do it?" Alyssa asked. "How did you get by?"

"We did a lot of things, child, but most of all, we sang. Let's all hold hands. I'll show you," Millie said softly.

We all joined hands around the table and stared intently at Millie. She closed her eyes and started to sing, and as she sang each new verse her voice got louder and louder. I closed my eyes too. I could feel the pain in her voice. I could feel the hurt and the suffering she endured. She sang the popular civil rights song "We Shall Overcome" made famous by Pete Seeger.

It was beautiful. Millie had a beautiful voice. I opened my eyes, and everyone was crying, to a person. We were all in tears. As Reggie would say, there was not a dry eye in the place. Surely, this would do the trick. Surely, this would settle the fight our two newly engaged neighbors had coming into this wonderful night of neighborly bonding. The air was cleared. Millie did that with her song.

Alyssa stood up to speak. "That was wonderful, Millie, but it's not me. I'm not ready to tell my family, and I guess that means I'm not ready to marry. Maybe someday I will overcome this, but that day is not today. I'm so sorry, Dawn."

Alyssa ran out of the house in tears. We all motioned for Dawn to follow her. She was reluctant, but she did leave to go after Alyssa. The storm passed over us all but it didn't dissipate, it just moved on. Millie's song shielded us, but it didn't shield Alyssa and Dawn. I guess not everybody could be spared.

We all looked at each other. We didn't quite know what to say. What was there to say, after all? I think Millie sang it all, and Alyssa was unmoved. In that moment, Millie spoke again. "They'll come around."

We all nodded our heads. Millie did it again. Her sage advice put us all at ease and the gathering could begin again. The food was great, and the dessert was even better. Ebony decided this event needed some alcohol to top it off. We all moved into the living room for some wine. A good after-dinner drink was just what the doctor ordered.

This seemed like a good time to ask for advice. I told everyone about what happened with Yolanda and with Tom. I was genuinely at a loss. Where should I go from here? What should we do next?

"Sometimes you just gotta let these things simmer," said Millie.

"I agree. Maybe if you take your focus off of this and put it on something more enjoyable, you'll be able to come back to this with a fresh outlook," Ebony said as she was motioning me toward Reggie.

"Nonsense," said Olivia. "As they say, the show must go on. You have to resolve this before you can move on. You need a new approach. You need a new suspect to look at. It was smart to look into Yolanda and Tom, and you might go back to either or both of them as you learn more, but you are ignoring an obvious lead."

"What do you mean?" I asked.

"Miss Millie did us all proud. That's a tough act to follow, but I think another song is in order. You can always learn a lot from Sondheim, in my opinion. He's a master of the spoken word. Here's what I mean."

Olivia cleared her throat, gulped a glass of water and stood on the coffee table. Every diva needs a stage, after all. Her being up on the table was a bit jarring at first, but for Olivia, it made sense. Then she started right in with her famous Broadway belt as she sang to a smashing finale. Her arms moved with passion, and you could hear the emotion in her voice. She knew how to please a crowd, but I didn't get it.

"I don't understand," I said.

Reggie piped in. He got it. "It's obvious: we are not focusing on the wife! She sang the song 'Could I Leave You?' From Sondheim's Follies. It's a song about a disgruntled wife."

"You got it, my friend," Olivia said with a smile. She was very proud of her performance. Obviously, she and Reggie were on the same page. Now that he said it, I felt a little silly for not having thought about looking more into Arthur's wife.

"You're right, Olivia," I said with gumption. "We need to pay Shanice a visit."

CHAPTER 23

IF AT FIRST YOU DON'T SUCCEED

Tania and I were hard at work. I was writing away. Tania was editing away. Majesta was sitting on my lap demanding I pet her head through it all. Majesta always made sure she got plenty of food and plenty of attention. Work has to get done, however boring that may sound. But just because you're doing work doesn't mean you can't find time for some girl talk.

"Last night was a whopper of a dinner," I said to Tania.

"I am a little jealous I don't get to do that dinner. Maybe you should invite a guest one of these days," Tania said.

"Maybe. It looks like Alyssa and Dawn have called off the wedding, and Olivia had a great idea about where we should go next, given that Yolanda has left town," I reported with enthusiasm.

"Sounds like a promising night. Sorry about Dawn and Alyssa. I liked Alyssa," Tania said with a sigh. "What's next on our agenda?"

"Olivia thought we should talk to Shanice again, and I think it's a good idea," I said. "The wife is always worth a look."

"Speaking of wives," Tania interrupted as she gave me a bossy stare.

"What about wives?" I asked inquisitively.

"You know what I mean!" she blasted. "Ever think of being one?"

"In order to be a wife, you need a groom," I shot back sharply.

"You have one next door, right?" Tania replied curtly.

Everyone was trying to set me up with Reggie. Last night I got it from Ebony, and today it was Tania's turn. What if I just don't want to get married? Besides, last time I thought Reggie was going to kiss me, it turned out to be a misrepresentation. In other words, I was wrong. It didn't happen.

"You know Reggie likes you!" Tania yelled.

"No, I don't!" I yelled back.

The loud noises angered poor Majesta, so she jumped off my lap. Good for me, because it was tough typing and petting her all at the same time. Before she jumped down, she looked at me and said she agreed with Tania. I was clearly outnumbered. No matter, I was used to being outnumbered. I was used to living on my own. That may seem lonely, but I'm my own boss, and I like it that way. I'm my own boss at home, and I'm my own boss at work, which I also do from home. When you think about it, everything comes back to my home for me. My home is my haven. My home is my starting point and my end point each day, and that's how I like it, quite frankly.

"Reggie hasn't said anything to me about his feelings for me. We just don't talk about that," I shared.

"Words are great, but sometimes actions are more important. You traffic in words, but words can hang you up. Sometimes words can be limiting. They can put you in a box that doesn't allow for much nuance," Tania said with the delivery of a prophet.

Just as she finished her thought, the front doorbell rang. It was Reggie.

"See what I mean, Sheila?" she said.

As always, Reggie was very excited. He was ready for another one of our little adventures. Maybe that's why he kept coming back, for the thrill of our next little excursion. Who knows?

"Did she tell you what happened last night?" Reggie asked Tania.

She nodded her head yes. Tania was also looking very excited and very sure of herself. She was hoping the prior conversation stuck with me.

"Well, then, let's be off. We need to talk to Shanice again."

We dutifully followed behind and got in his car. I guess we had nothing to lose. What's the worst thing that could happen? This was surely a win-win. We share what we know, and we get more inside information from Shanice. That was clearly how this was going to go.

We got to the house, rang the doorbell, and nobody answered. I guess that's what could happen too. She's not home. We were left at the altar by Shanice, so to speak, and I was not about to be left at the altar literally. The thought of me getting married was insane. And Reggie being the guy was even more wacky. We weren't even dating, and my friends were trying to get us married.

I sharply turned around to go back to the car. "Well, this is a bust," I said. "We have work to do anyway. We'll try back later, I guess."

Reggie grabbed my arm and waved no with his pointer finger. "She might be back soon," he said. "We can't leave just yet. Let's wait a little bit. Maybe she is on her way home."

As if on cue, her car pulled up to the driveway. She was back. She looked distracted. Shanice was joyous. Obviously, someone had a good night. She was smiling and whistling as she maneuvered her house key. When she brought her head back up to eye level, she saw us waiting at her front door.

"How can I help you guys?" she asked.

"We just wanted to chat again," I said.

"Really, about what?" She looked genuinely confused. I guess if I were her, I would be confused too. This woman just recently lost her husband, and these strangers kept popping up asking more and more questions. As a journalist, questions are my thing, so it was sometimes hard for me to understand why other people despised them so much. Grieving widows get a pass, I guess.

"We were just in the area, and we thought we would pay you a visit," Reggie said politely.

"How kind of you all," Shanice responded. She was still very distracted and uncomfortable, but I could tell she didn't want to be dismissive or rude.

"Yeah, we're just hanging around," Tania said awkwardly.

I don't think "hanging around" was the best turn of phrase in this situation. "Honestly, I just can't get your husband out of my mind. I just have to know more about him," I said. "What was he like? What made him tick?"

This line of questioning was going nowhere. Shanice seemed more and more distant. She was not engaging at all. In fact, she was disengaging. She started rustling through her purse, looking for something.

"You had your keys a minute ago," I said.

"I did, but I was looking for something else," Shanice pointed out. "I must have left it at my friend's house."

"What is it? What are you missing, exactly?" I asked.

"Just something important; well, something important to me," Shanice said. "I have to be going. Thanks for stopping by. I'll see you again soon, maybe. Bye."

She turned around and got back in her car and drove off, leaving the three of us at her doorstep. That was weird, for sure. Who does that? She obviously did not want to talk to us at all.

I walked back to the car thinking this was over now, but this time Tania stopped me. It was unavoidable; my friends just didn't want me to leave this woman's house. So I went along again. "What's up, Tania?" I asked.

"Last time, you caught Yolanda in a telling conversation when you snooped around the back of her house. Maybe we should poke around before we leave," Tania noted.

"It can't hurt," Reggie added.

I went along for the ride. They were right, what could it hurt? So we went around the side of the house. There was nothing to see, and we knew Shanice was out, so we were not going to overhear another call. I wanted to go back to the car at this point, but Tania and Reggie ran ahead. I followed.

The back of the house did not have a deck. The back door was locked, of course, but Tania noticed a window slightly open above, on the second floor. She pointed to the open window madly. I shrugged my shoulders, confused.

"That window is open," she said. "Maybe I can get in."

"How, exactly?" I asked.

"I'll boost her up," Reggie said.

This had bad written all over it. I just had a bad feeling. You know those kinds of feelings? They come over you all of a sudden and you just shake your head. Of course, Reggie and Tania were not listening. Before I could object, Tania was trying to climb on Reggie's back. Tania was slim, but Reggie still could not hold her weight. I knew what was going to happen next. They looked like an old tree that was ready to give up. Reggie's back was creaking. He moved his hand to rub off the pain, which shifted his body, and Tania fell to the ground, landing on her left arm. She screamed in pain. I didn't laugh; I quickly ran to her side.

The neighbor must have heard us because a woman came around back, asking us what we were doing. We were at a loss, so all three of us just ran as quickly as we could back to Reggie's car and got Tania to the emergency room. Thankfully, nothing was broken, but she did have a sprain. They gave her an arm brace and not a cast.

I shook my head again in disbelief. It was just another epic fail in a long list of epic fails. "So what do we do next?" I asked.

Reggie answered, "We go back."

"What?" I said, shocked.

"Why so shocked?" Tania asked. "Shanice never answered your questions, so we go back again tomorrow, and the day after that, until she does."

"Exactly," Reggie said in total agreement.

I guessed they were right. We didn't get answers, so we should keep pushing. Shanice didn't seem as closed off as Yolanda, so maybe she would talk more, eventually, if we were persistent.

So we went back the next day and she wasn't there. We went back the day after that, and she wasn't there. We went back yet again the day after that, and she still was not there. Finally, on the fourth day we went back, we saw her car was back in the driveway. I wondered where she was for four days. I wondered what we would learn from finally getting to question her. I wondered if she'd let us more fully question her at all.

We rang the doorbell and when she answered to see us at the other end, she was clearly annoyed this time around. The niceties had all but gone away. Shanice was openly frustrated with us at this point.

"What is going on?" she asked.

"We just want to talk," I said.

"You always want to talk. You will never leave me alone, it seems," she barked at us. "What have I done to you to deserve this? When will you just stop and go away?"

"I'm so sorry for all this, but we still think your husband was murdered," I said.

As I finished my statement, the neighbor came from next door, pointing at us wildly, saying, "Those are the people I saw breaking into your house!"

"This has to end!" Shanice cried. "I am trying to be polite to you people, but you won't listen. I'm done answering your questions. The police say my husband was mugged. I don't know why you won't leave this alone, but I have to just move on."

We were clearly too tough on her. She was cracking up before our eyes. I felt bad for her. This was too much for a grieving widow to endure. We just had to back off. So I apologized, and we went back to Reggie's car. We could all see Shanice slam the door shut in anger.

"I think we've been too harsh," I said.

"Nonsense, she's got a guilty conscience over something. Why won't she just talk to us?" Reggie said. He was staring intently at Shanice's house. His eyes were laser-focused on the front door.

"What are you so fascinated about?" I asked.

"Don't you see? She's upset, just like Yolanda was when we confronted her," Reggie explained.

"What does that matter?" I asked.

"Yeah, what does that matter?" Tania echoed.

"This is when they get sloppy and do something stupid or call for help," Reggie said.

"I don't think so," I replied.

"Wait for it," he insisted.

Sure enough, Reggie was right. Moments later, a car pulled into Shanice's driveway. It was a familiar car too. Out of the car came Tom. He rang the doorbell and Shanice answered. She had been crying. Her makeup was running. Tom took her in his arms and held her tight. The sudden move shocked all three of us, but that's not all that shocked us.

He kissed her, and it wasn't just a friendly kiss, it was a passionate kiss. Shanice and Tom were more than friends. I don't kiss my friends like that. Shanice and Tom were clearly lovers. Now, at long last, we were finally getting somewhere. As the old saying goes, if at first you don't succeed, try, try again.

CHAPTER 24
EXPOSING SECRETS

Our jaws were practically on the ground. We could not believe what we saw. Shanice, Arthur's wife, was obviously having an affair with Tom, Arthur's friend and Yolanda's business partner. This was big! This was huge! But before we got too far ahead of ourselves, we had to be careful. We didn't want to jump to conclusions. We had to ask ourselves: when did they get together? How serious is this relationship? Does this at all connect to Arthur's murder?

Grieving people need comforting. Losing your spouse is a massive, life-changing event. Not that I would know, but I could guess. When we first saw Shanice, she was upset. She seemed like the typical wife that was devastated over the death of her husband. Was it all an act? Maybe Tom and Shanice connected over their shared grief after Arthur passed away. It was possible.

Reggie was literally jumping up and down in his seat. He was surely convinced this was an affair that stretched on to before Arthur was killed. I could tell he thought Shanice was far from innocent. Similarly, Tania just sat in the back seat with her hand over her mouth. You could sense she was clearly taken aback by what she saw. Someone had to focus the group and, of course, that responsibility rested with me.

"Let's focus, people," I said. "What did we just see? What just happened? Did we see a broken-up wife move on with her husband's best friend or have they been together for a long, long time?"

"Did you see that kiss?" Reggie asked.

"I saw it, but what does it mean, exactly?" I probed.

"It means Shanice and Tom are an item, that's for sure," Reggie answered.

"Clearly. But when did this love connection start?" I pushed back at Reggie.

"Regardless of when, it's going hot and heavy now," he replied.

Our little banter was cut short because Tom and Shanice were exiting the house hand in hand. They got in Tom's car together and drove off.

"Enough with the hypotheticals, people, let's follow them," instructed Tania.

Reggie agreed and off we went. We were following Tom and Shanice as they drove through town. They weren't in a hurry. They were on a joy ride.

"Maybe they're off to the bank," Reggie theorized.

"Why?" I asked.

"To get their hands on Arthur's safety deposit box so they can take his money and follow Yolanda off into the sunset."

"I think that's a bit dramatic," I countered. "Besides, we don't know Arthur even had a safety deposit box."

"They all have safety deposit boxes," Reggie said.

Well, this conversation was going nowhere. Reggie was letting his overactive imagination get away with him. He had clearly watched too many movies and seen too many plays. Based on the frantic conversations I overheard the morning of Arthur's death, it seemed to me like he was looking for money, not hoarding it. Regardless, Reggie was cute. Anytime he came up with a new theory, his eyes just lit up. It was like he was coming alive, and that was a pleasant sight to see, at least for me, anyway.

"I think maybe it's time to call Anthony," I said.

"Why?" Reggie asked.

"We should tell him what we saw."

"We didn't see anything worth calling the police about. You just called him when we cornered Yolanda in the airport as security was trying to escort us away, and that turned out to be nothing. Do you really want to call him again?" Reggie asked with a twinge of anger in his voice.

"I think you're right," I admitted. "We should hold off. I don't want him to think I'm the boy who cried wolf, after all."

"We certainly can't have that," he said sarcastically.

Once again, Reggie's anger toward Anthony was showing its ugly face. Anthony took me seriously as a reporter. He was a good source and always worked with me, even if the other police officers dismissed me. He always had a way of making me feel valued.

"I know where he's headed," Tania said.

"Where?" I asked.

"Look familiar?" She pointed ahead of us. "It's the restaurant he took me to for lunch. He must like it here. I guess he takes all his girl-friends here."

Tania didn't miss a beat. She was right. It was indeed the same restaurant. This might not be the best location for us to confront Shan-ice, after what happened here last time. Hopefully, I wouldn't get slapped and doused with water again. We would have to navigate this situation carefully. We'd avoided spending the night in jail so far, but this could be the thing that got us a one-way ticket to the slammer.

Tom and Shanice entered the restaurant hand in hand. They were not hiding their affection. They shared another kiss as they entered the restaurant. Some people have no shame, no shame at all. That woman's husband just died and here she was, kissing his friend. Surely, she could have waited at least a year to move on. I guess Arthur wasn't as great a husband as he appeared, or maybe Shanice wasn't as great a wife.

"Let's get going," Reggie said anxiously. "If we confront them when they are together, they'll be caught off guard."

"Hold on, tiger," I said. "Remember what happened last time we were here?"

"So what?" he answered. "This is different."

Reggie jumped out of the car and sprinted toward the restaurant. Tania and I ran after him. He was a man on a mission. I liked this take-charge Reggie. He was just as determined as I was to solve this murder. He was all in.

However, as I suspected, we were stopped at the door. The host would not let us in. Our reputations preceded us, and they were having none of it.

"You are not going to make another scene in this establishment," the host said.

"You can't do this to us! You can't treat us this way! We have to get in there!" Reggie shouted back. I didn't think arguing with the man was the best approach.

"Make no mistake, if you enter this restaurant, I will call the police," the host said flatly.

And there you have it. We were excommunicated from this restaurant. I didn't know how I felt about that, knowing there was a restaurant in town I was literally banned from going to. So we quickly regrouped in the car. Tania suggested we try getting in again, but this time use some of Reggie's costumes to see if we could get past the host.

We searched through Reggie's stash. Posing as police got us nowhere at the airport, so we had to try something new. Besides, we couldn't just flash a badge. The host would still know it was us. We needed something that would make us look unrecognizable. This costume had to make us look like we were completely different people.

Playing dress-up was new to me. As a child, I was not big on make-believe games. I have always been rooted in truth. I guess that's why I became a journalist. Seeking truth is what we do, after all. It's who we are at our core. Every good journalist wants to get to the bottom of the story and get to the heart of the matter.

We found just the right costumes. We put on cowboy hats, and Reggie also put on a fake mustache. We looked like people straight out of the South. I thought I would never be caught dead in a cowboy hat, but here we were.

As we approached the host, we thought we were going to get in for sure. We were slick.

The host greeted us. "Nice hats," he said with a smile. "Who exactly do you think you're fooling with this?"

"Whatever do you mean?" Tania said in her best Southern accent.

He proceeded to take off our hats and throw them on the ground. The host was not violent or rude. It was a calm unmasking, but an unmasking it was, nonetheless. "Now, please take your hats and go," he advised.

As directed, we went back to the car, defeated and exposed. Regardless of the humiliation, we were not going to let this stop us from moving forward with our plan to interrogate Shanice and Tom while they were out and about together. Instead of continuing with our little game of dress-up, we decided to just wait in the car for them to leave the restaurant, and we would stop them before they entered Tom's car. The plan was simple enough to work without us getting into any further trouble.

As if on cue, Tom and Shanice left the restaurant. Again, they shared a kiss. All of these public displays of affection were getting to be a lot. Who does that, anyway? I guess couples do. Close couples. Couples that were clearly very comfortable with each other. The more I saw Shanice and Tom together, the more I became convinced, as Reggie was, they were not a young couple; they were a couple with a history.

Seeing them together did get me thinking. If I was in a relationship, would I behave that way? Surely not. I've been around the block, so to speak, and I have never behaved that way. It seems almost undignified, I think. In my life, I have been called a lot of things by a lot of people, but nobody has ever accused me of being undignified. I'm proud of that, actually. No matter how many insults or put-downs came my way, I always seemed to rise above. I might have been knocked down for a minute, but never more than a minute.

Before Tom and Shanice could get in the car, we were there waiting for them. There was no escaping us. Tom and Shanice knew us well by this point. They both stopped in their tracks. I could see the guilt all over their faces. They knew they were caught. They knew they were in a compromising position they could not just explain away, but Shanice was still going to try.

"I was just meeting my good friend Tom for lunch," she said. "We have really bonded after Arthur's death."

"Yes, it's been a hard time for both of us, but we are getting through it together," Tom said. "Unlike you three, we are not stalking people and harassing them."

"Cut the crap!" Tania said. "You had your eyes on my cleavage the whole time I was your secretary. I remember you taking me to this restaurant not too long ago."

"What is she talking about, Tom?" Shanice asked defensively.

"She was my secretary for a day, and she does not know what she's talking about," Tom responded.

"Let's forget Tania. We saw you two kissing multiple times. We know you're more than friends, so you can just quit the act," Reggie said with authority.

Tom and Shanice knew they were caught at this point, and trying to talk their way out of the situation was just not going to happen. They were going to have to tell the truth, or at least their version of the truth. Shanice, for one, knew she was outmatched. She had tried to dodge us and left her house for four whole days, no doubt playing house with Tom. Regardless, she couldn't slip away. We were not going to let her escape like Yolanda.

"Okay, what do you want to know?" Shanice asked.

"What's really going on here?" I asked.

"The marriage was over, and Arthur knew it, but he was still trying to keep me in his good graces. He thought he could trick me into staying. I'd just had enough," Shanice said.

"Arthur was a friend, but he was always up to something. He was always looking for a get-rich-quick scheme. It was just too much," Tom added.

"So you two had to get him out of the way so you could be together?" Reggie asked.

"No, that's not how it was at all," Shanice said. "I talked to him the morning of his death. I was trying to tell him the marriage was over, but he insisted he had some big plan he was working on and everything was going to work out great this time. We all know how that ended."

"Yes, with Arthur dead," I said firmly. "I did overhear a conversation like that. He also talked to his mother; you know, your biggest client-slash-partner, Tom."

"Yolanda keeps me very comfortable. I help her manage her money and her properties. I am helping her sell some properties right now, and I'm going to get a nice cut," Tom reported.

"I can place the conversation Arthur had with you, Shanice, and the one he had with his mother, but there was a third conversation," I noted. "He was at that deli to meet someone. Was that person you, Tom?"

"It most certainly was not," Tom said. "Maybe it's the person that murdered him, if he was even murdered at all. Just a bit of advice, you should probably find out who that caller was."

Tom and Shanice got in the car and drove off. They had surely given me a lot to think about. Who was that third caller? Why did that person agree to meet Arthur at the deli that morning? What was Arthur's plan? All these questions and so many more were going through my head. Arthur and his family sure had a lot of secrets. Some we had already gotten to the bottom of, but there were more to come, I felt. There was more to know, and I was determined to know everything.

CHAPTER 25
MOMMA KNOWS BEST

Today began like any other day. I was dreaming away about capturing Arthur's murderer. I was in a dark house tracking the murderer. The killer ran into the house, all dressed in black so I couldn't see their face. The sky was gray and downcast as I followed the killer into the old house, which resembled something in an old-fashioned horror movie, but being the intrepid reporter I am, I was not going to let my fear overcome me. I was going in.

The floorboards creaked as I stepped in the old house. I felt a chill across my shoulders. In that moment, up ahead, I saw the killer run around the corner into a room, so I gave chase. Once in the room, the killer's back was toward me. I still couldn't see his or her face at all. This was the moment of the big reveal.

"Stop, it's over!" I shouted at the killer.

Despite my command, the killer did not respond or even move at all. So I grabbed the killer by the arm and swung them around so I could see their face. It was horrible. It was monstrous. Just like the three-headed dog, Cerberus, that protects the underworld, the killer had three heads: Yolanda, Shanice, and Tom, all in one person, on one body. I screamed out of fear and woke up out of my dream.

As I sat up in my bed, there was Majesta, sitting on my stomach, shaking her head in disapproval.

"You had one of those dreams again, didn't you?" she asked with a slightly judgmental tone.

"Yes, but I'm okay," I answered.

At that response, she purred and came up to my face. She rubbed her face across my cheek lovingly. Majesta might be a demanding cat, but she's all mine, and we love each other. Yes, I said it, I love my cat, and I am not ashamed! It's okay to love your pet like a friend or companion. Ever since I found her at my doorstep, it was clear she was meant for me.

Just like any other morning, my next step was to go down to the kitchen to feed Majesta and start my day. As I went down the stairs, something was very different. I smelled butter and blueberries and coffee in the air. It was such a pleasant, welcoming smell. It was also a very comforting and familiar smell for me. It was the smell of week-ends with Momma.

There she was, cooking away in my kitchen. My mother had a key to my house, which she used whenever she needed it. She was a mother hen, always protecting her young and speaking her mind at every step of the way. A typical Italian mom, she was very protective of me and my younger brother. My mom only stood about five feet, four inches tall, but she was a larger-than-life figure. Don't be fooled by her short, curly, brown hair and her round cheeks, she was not to be played with. Her name is Sue, but me and my brother, Johnnie, just call her Momma, and everyone else calls her Momma Sue because she was not just our momma, she was Momma to everyone that came in contact with her.

"Great to see you, Momma!" I said as I went to hug her. When I was hugging my Momma, all was right with the world. I knew I was loved and safe.

"I am fine, my sweet girl. I just had to stop by and check in on you."

"Things are good, Momma, but they are even better now."

"Have you talked to your brother?"

"Yes, we talked last week. He seems fine. He promised me it would just take one more semester for him to finish this degree, and, of course, he needed some money to tide himself over. I sent it to him," I answered lovingly. Johnnie was a dreamer—always switching majors and never settling.

"I talked to him too, but he didn't ask me for anything," she said. "If he needed money, he should have asked me."

"I think he thought he would give you a break," I responded.

"Nonsense, I'm his momma, that's my job."

"How is Swanky-ville treating you?" I asked.

My momma only lived about an hour away from me, in a very rich town. We jokingly called it Swanky-ville. When I was ten, my dad left. We never knew why, he just left. Mind you, his relationship with my mother wasn't perfect, but we didn't see it coming. He left a note wishing the three of us well, but said he felt suffocated and had to get away from his life with us. My mom and brother were devastated. I never got along that well with him, so I think I took it the best.

From there, my mom had to support us on her own. She sometimes worked two or three jobs at a time. Regardless, she was always there for us. She made it all work. Suddenly, three years ago, she reconnected with her sister, Ida. My mom and dad had eloped, so she was estranged from her family. My grandparents passed away, and it was just my mom and her sister left. In that time, Ida apparently married rich because when she and my mom reconnected, Aunt Ida had a lot of money and a big house in Swanky-ville. About a year ago, Aunt Ida died of lung cancer. She was a big smoker. That's when my mom's life changed, at least financially. My aunt Ida had no kids, so she left everything to my mom, and now my mom was living in the big Swanky-ville house with enough money to quit her many jobs.

"Everything is great!" Momma said, but I could tell she wasn't happy. All those jobs kept her busy, and when she wasn't working, she was obsessing over me and Johnnie. Now she was alone in a big house with a lot of money and no one to share it all with. So she would randomly show up at my house when she was lonely or bored, and I would welcome her with open arms.

"Let's go in the living room and eat," I said.

"I was looking at that living room of yours. Those sofas are getting worn. You and I need to go buy some new ones," she said.

"Of course, Momma."

Just as we got to the living room, the front doorbell rang and it was Tania. She smelled the blueberries instantly and walked right past me. How do you like that, my best friend and copy editor not even saying hi as she enters my house? The smell was overpowering and pleasant, which I guess counted more than saying hello to me.

Once Tania saw my mom, the two hugged lovingly. In college, Tania was on academic probation one year, so she spent a summer with us because things were tense for her at her house. That summer, Tania became my mom's "second daughter," of sorts. The two became instant friends. My mom was most comfortable when she was, well, mothering, and Tania needed a lot of mothering.

"I've missed you, Momma Sue," Tania said.

"I'm just an hour away. You need to stop by," my mom replied. After that, she twirled Tania around and looked at her closely. She was clearly inspecting her. "You've lost weight. You're getting too skinny. Sheila, you are not paying her enough. You need to give Tania a raise so she can get more food in that belly of hers."

"I've just been on a diet, that's all," Tania said.

"Well, it's working too well, and you need to go back to eating," my mom responded. "Luckily, I made blueberry pancakes so you can start eating up right now."

"They smell amazing!" Tania said.

My mom smiled uncontrollably. She looked like the Cheshire cat. My mom loves cooking and getting compliments on her cooking. She can do anything in the kitchen except bake. Feeding others is like food to my mom's soul. It keeps her going. It's all just a part of that mothering thing she does so well.

"Did Sheila tell you what we've been doing?" Tania asked.

I stared at Tania disapprovingly. She realized in that moment I had not discussed it with my mom and did not want to either. Regardless, there was no getting out of it now. We had to tell her everything. She was not going to give in until she knew, and I wasn't about to lie.

Once my mom heard I had witnessed a murder, she went into overdrive asking me all these questions—see where I get the whole questioning thing? She was beside herself. She had to know every detail and everything we'd been through. There was no stopping her now; she was involved, and she was not going to be satisfied until she knew everything.

"It's been a lot to deal with, Momma, but we are handling it," I said.

"Nonsense, you need your momma here to help. I'm not leaving until this is over. Luckily for you, I brought some clothes. I'll be staying right here with you for the next few days," she declared forcefully.

I could see that coming up with a reason to stay was going to happen regardless, and there was no sense fighting it. Who packs some clothes when they visit their daughter if they were not intending to stay? It was fine, though. I thought I'd like having my mom around for a little while. It would be like old times.

The doorbell rang again, and this time it was Reggie. I got up to answer it, but by the time I was halfway there, my mom was already at the door welcoming him in.

"There's a cute guy at the door, Sheila!" she hollered.

Of course, I was mortified. Reggie looked a bit red in the face as well, but he was happy to be called cute for sure. The problem with my mom is she has no filter, really. Everything that comes into her head just comes out of her mouth. Sometimes it can be cute, and other times, most times, it is just embarrassing.

"This is my new neighbor, Reggie, Momma," I said.

"Call me Momma Sue; that's what everyone calls me. How long have you known my daughter?" she asked.

"Pleased to meet you, Momma Sue. I just moved in next door. It's only been a few weeks," Reggie replied.

There she goes with the questions again. Reggie smiled. He could see where I got my inquisitive nature right away. I thought he'd fit in great with my mom. Now that I think about it, who doesn't fit in great with my mom? It's hard being universally loved, but she pulls it off with ease.

Majesta came into the living room and jumped on my lap. She seemed very mad. Of course, with all the visitors, I forgot to feed her.

"Feed that cat too. She's also looking a little skinny," my mom said.

Majesta looked up at me and purred in agreement, so off I went to the kitchen while my mother held court in the living room with Reggie and Tania. She was in her element, striking up conversation and laughing. I was now even more convinced that having her stay for a while would be a big positive for everyone, even Reggie.

After feeding Majesta, I went back into the living room and was greeted by a few more questions.

"Reggie tells me he is also a writer. Do you know he writes about theater?" my mom asked.

"Yes, Momma, I know what Reggie does," I answered.

"So why haven't you hired him to write for you? That online paper of yours is all about news. You could use some lighter coverage. Everyone loves the theater," she said.

"Momma Sue, I knew I was going to like you the minute I saw you," Reggie said.

"Of course you're going to like me, what's not to like? We're going to be fast friends," my mom pointed out.

"Reggie has been trying to convince me to expand the paper," I said.

"You should listen to him and your momma," she responded.

Luckily, my mom left it at that. Reggie and I had discussed the topic on and off, but I wasn't convinced it was right for the publication. I started the publication to analyze the latest news. I just wasn't sure adding a theater or entertainment component was best for what I wanted to do with it. It was still a thought I was considering, and Reggie kept bringing up.

With that, we got back to business, discussing the murder of Arthur. Reggie told my mom he was helping out, which made him even more amazing in her eyes. Johnnie was always her favorite because he needed more care than me. I was always more independent. So my mom gave me enough space to let me do my own thing, but was sure to give me her opinion when she had an opinion to share, and she often had an opinion to share.

We were alone in the kitchen together when she cornered me. "That man is so nice, Sheila. He's a keeper, and he likes you."

"Do you really think so, Momma?"

"I know so, and based on how you look at him, I think you like him too. You know, you aren't getting any younger," she pointed out.

"I just met the man, Momma," I said. We both smiled and shared a quick hug before going back to the living room.

Once we were all together in the room, my mom made an announcement. She declared, "Momma knows best; I'm definitely staying to help you guys solve this murder."

CHAPTER 26
THE WRONG MAN

I t was settled. My mother was staying, and she was going to "help" us solve this murder. Don't get me wrong, my momma can be very helpful, but sometimes it doesn't work out the way she planned it would. Good intentions don't always result in good outcomes.

For example, bake sales are common in school, as we all know. I loved the bake sales because we got to eat new treats we didn't usually get. I'm a bit of a foodie. I like trying new foods and flavors. My momma's cupcakes were indeed a new flavor. She was determined to contribute to the bake sale, so she decided to bake strawberry cupcakes. Clearly, baking was not the thing that was going to make my momma shine.

At first, the cupcakes more closely resembled oatmeal, in that they were still liquid and lumpy. But my momma did not stop there. She decided they just needed more time in the oven. After more time in the oven, they came out a toasty brown, and I do mean toasty, because they more closely resembled burnt toast than cupcakes. The effort was great, but the outcome was not so great. My momma means well.

The doorbell rang, and I went to open it only to be totally shocked when I saw Lieutenant Crooks on my doorstep. Words don't describe how much grief and trouble this man has put me through. He is literally the devil without the horns and red skin and all that.

My mom followed behind me because she just has to be in the center of it all. She can't be an afterthought or sit back. I was speechless. I was staring at Crooks, but I just couldn't talk. I didn't know what to say, and honestly, part of me just wanted to slam the door in his face.

"Who is it, dear?" Momma Sue asked. I didn't responded. I was still silent. My momma could see I was frozen, so she pushed me aside. "How can I help you?"

"You don't know how long I've waited to see you speechless," Crooks said sarcastically.

"Excuse me!" Momma Sue responded. "This is my daughter you are talking to!"

"I'm so sorry," he continued with a snicker. "I have not one, but two restraining orders against you, Sheila. I suggest you stay far away from Shanice and Tom, or not, in which case, I will have to arrest you."

Crooks could not contain his joy. He was smiling bright. Clearly, this encounter made his day.

"You had to deliver these yourself?" I asked. Finally, I was able to say something to him.

"Are you crazy? I wouldn't miss this for the world," he chuckled in response. Crooks was having a grand old time while I was mortified. The fact that my actions were giving him a certain satisfaction was enough for me to snap out of it. I had never been visited by the police before. As a reporter, I visited them often, but the favor was never returned, until today.

"I have no intention of visiting Tom or Shanice again, thank you," I said defiantly.

"That's a shame, I would love to be the officer that enforces these restraining orders. Although, I have to admit, delivering them is very satisfying in and of itself. After years of being on the other end of your questions, it is a bit fulfilling to be here at your doorstep on official business."

My momma had had just about enough of Crooks. She was like a teakettle, and her water had boiled long enough and was now just waiting to whistle away. Well, the wait was over.

"Again, how dare you talk to my daughter this way?" she shouted. "Sheila is a good reporter. No, Sheila is a *great* reporter. And if she got in your face, it was because you deserved it. I have never been in the presence of such an unprofessional police officer in all my life. If this is how you address the public, you should find yourself another line of work."

I'm not sure Crooks had ever been spoken to like this before because now he was silent. My momma had shut him up right quick. He was not going to talk to me or anyone else like that again anytime soon, I was willing to bet. This was surely the end of the road for Crooks's horrible attitude. Well, maybe not the end of the road entirely, but at least the end of the road today.

"Furthermore, my daughter witnessed a murder, and all you've done is dismiss her!" my momma continued. "She has told me everything. You are a disgrace! Instead of harassing my daughter, you should be out there trying to hunt down the murderers!"

"I do apologize for my rudeness," Crooks said, sweet as pie. He knew he was wrong to be so nasty with me. "In the matter of Arthur's murder, we are still convinced it was a mugging gone wrong, and there will be more developments to this end shortly. Have a great day."

Crooks left with his tail between his legs. It was great to see him shamed. He deserved it.

As we went back to the living room, I couldn't get it out of my head that he felt "more developments" were coming. Had they found Arthur's murderers?

Tania and Reggie were curious about what just happened at the front door. Once they heard about the restraining order, they were very distraught. It was nice to have a bunch of supportive friends around me. Witnessing a murder sure takes a lot out of you, but endeavoring to solve said murder is even worse. Some days I felt so determined to move forward, and other days I felt conflicted. Although, I have to say, the days I was filled with the desire to solve this murder far outweighed those days when I thought I was in a little bit over my head.

As we all settled in after the visit from Lieutenant Crooks, you guessed it, the doorbell rang again. My house was just the place to visit today! This time, Reggie was quick to get up. He didn't want to see another confrontation happen in front of my house.

"I'm going to get the door this time," he said. "If it's Crooks, I'll just send him away."

"What do you mean? This is my house, so I should get it," I said.

"Let Reggie handle this one, Sheila," Momma Sue said gently but firmly. I yielded. As Reggie went off to get the door, my momma said, "I'm telling you, Sheila, this one is a keeper."

I could hear a familiar voice. It wasn't Crooks. I had to admit, I was relieved, but Reggie was not. It was Anthony. Reggie reluctantly invited Anthony in, and once he entered the living room, my mother stood up.

"My daughter did nothing wrong," Momma Sue said. "I don't know why you police officers seem to enjoy visiting today, but you can just turn around and go back to the station, or wherever you work."

"It's okay, Momma. He's a good one," I said. Reggie rolled his eyes in disapproval. I saw Reggie's reaction, but chose to ignore it. Anthony was welcome; he was a friend, of sorts.

"I have news, Sheila," Anthony said. "But first, I wanted to tell you how sorry I am about the restraining order. Crooks insisted on delivering it. I've never seen him so happy."

"He's gone. No worries. I don't plan on violating any order," I assured Anthony. He seemed relieved. I could see his body and overall demeanor get lighter. Obviously, he thought I was going to wrestle my way back into Tom's office or Shanice's house, but I thought we were done with that. Besides, those efforts got us nowhere.

"That man was horrible," Momma Sue reported. "He should be fired from the force. He treated Sheila like dirt, and nobody treats my daughter like dirt! I told him off right quick! That man was obviously never disciplined as a child because he became real quiet after I told him what to do with himself."

Anthony laughed. "I would have liked to see that," he said. "The real reason I'm here is to tell you they have a suspect. They think they have found the man that mugged Arthur in the alley. Of course, they think he killed him too."

"That's great!" I cried with joy. I think I literally jumped for joy. "But if they have someone, they should have called me to identify him."

"Well, they don't want you involved, but I think you should talk to this guy. You are a witness, after all," Anthony noted. He was a good cop for sure. Anthony wanted to make sure justice was served here. So I left my mom, Reggie, and Sheila at home and followed Anthony back to his car and we drove to the station. Maybe the police did their jobs and all this was soon to be over, I thought and hoped.

As I drove in the car with Anthony, there was a sense of dread coming over me. Why? you might ask. Because if they didn't get the right guy, what was I going to do? Also, there was a woman on Arthur's back helping the man beat him, so even if this was the guy, there was still a woman out there that also had some responsibility. What happens in that case? How do I tell them they got the guy, but there's another bad person out there to look for? Surely, that was not going to go over well.

Anthony led me to a room where you could visit prisoners. I was told to wait and they would bring the man out. I can't lie, I was nervous. In fact, I was a nervous wreck. I was just waiting, and waiting, what seemed like hours but was probably just minutes. I'm a very impatient person. Waiting is not a strong point for me, I openly admit.

He was led out in handcuffs, and the police officers pushed him forward. He was distracted. He was looking around everywhere but at me. He also looked to me like he was talking to himself. Was this the man? Was this the murderer?

He sat down on the other side of the glass and picked up the phone. He looked me straight in the eye for the first time. He did not have two different eye colors like the murderer. However, maybe the two eye colors were because of the way the sun was hitting his face and not because he actually had two different eye colors. Maybe I was wrong about that.

"They are coming for me," he said, whispering.

"Who is coming for you?" I asked.

"The aliens are coming for me. Ever since I first saw them, the police have been stalking me. The police must be working with the aliens. They want to keep me quiet," the disturbed man said. He was clearly paranoid, nervous, and afraid. I was both shocked and amused by his story. Who doesn't want to prove the existence of aliens? Well, maybe not everyone longs to report on aliens, but it has always been a story that intrigued me, personally. It seems very arrogant on our part to assume we are the only sentient life in the universe. But I digress. We're not here to talk about aliens.

"Do you remember killing Arthur in the alley near Harry's?" I asked.

"I love Harry's. The food there is great, especially the bagels. Harry is a nice man. He's a prophet. He talks to me about life and how to be a better person. I like Harry. He's a prophet. He talks to me kindly," the suspected murderer said.

"I like Harry too. He's a dear friend and a good man," I said. The man nodded his head in agreement. This guy had a beard but it was shorter, and had more gray. I wish I got a better look at the murderer's face, but I only saw him for a second. I'm ashamed I don't remember his face. Also, when we saw him give Yolanda the envelope, we only saw him from behind. Maybe asking about Yolanda was a better approach.

"Do you remember delivering the envelope to Yolanda?" I asked.

"I remember going to Harry's in the morning. Everyone was inside. Some guy knocked into me before the police grabbed him. I think he saw aliens too. He must have seen aliens. Why else would they be beating on him so hard when he didn't do anything wrong?"

Now everything became clearer to me. This man was a frequent visitor to Harry's. I'm sure he went there often; that's why the police picked him up. Now the poor guy was being accused of murder, and he was understandably afraid. He was also obviously a little problemed, if you know what I mean. But this man did not kill Arthur at all; in fact, he was a witness to the murder, just like me. The police were never going to believe his story if he continued to talk about aliens, so it was still up to me to solve this murder.

CHAPTER 27
AN IMPORTANT MEMORY

O n the ride back home, I told Anthony about how my
meeting with the suspect went. It was a relief to have
someone that would listen to me at the police station
when so many there were so confrontational. As a reporter, we're
always asking questions. Our job is to second-guess just about
everything. You can't take anything at face value in my line of
work. I understand that can make me seem like a problem to some.
People don't like being questioned. People don't like being
challenged.

Putting all of that aside, Anthony was different. He was open-
minded, and able to take constructive criticism. You have to be secure
within yourself to be able to deal with constant questions coming from
us reporters because if you're not, those feelings of inadequacy show
their ugly head. In the end, reporters are people too, and we have a job
to do; that's all. It's not personal—well, most of the time, it's not
personal.

"I don't think he's the guy," I said.

"Why would you say that?" Anthony asked.

"If you really listen to him and get past all the talk of aliens, he
admitted to me he saw the police officers grab Arthur and beat him in

the alley. Well, I mean the murderers dressed as police officers," I continued.

"We'll keep looking into it, but I can't keep Crooks from making an arrest," Anthony pointed out.

"I know, but I also know you'll do your best," I noted. "Besides, I saw a man and a woman, not just a man, attacking Arthur. Also, I saw the male murderer give Yolanda a package, and this guy didn't even know who Yolanda was."

"Again, I'll do my best to keep Crooks at bay, but they really want to wrap this one up," Anthony said as we pulled into my driveway. There was a moving truck behind us that followed us into the cul-de-sac. I couldn't help staring at it. "It looks like someone is moving," Anthony noted

"Oh no, that moving van is going to Dawn's house," I said.

Anthony dropped me off at my front door in a very gentlemanly manner, which I appreciated. My mom, Reggie, and Tania had enough police today, so I told him I would let myself in. Anthony understood and drove off. Before I could go back in the house, I heard loud crying. I turned to see Dawn open her door in tears.

So, being a good neighbor, I went over there to console her. I suspected Alyssa was moving out after the altercation at dinner. I really liked Alyssa, and hoped this wasn't permanent. Maybe I could turn things around and be an encouraging voice of reason. Relationships are hard. You have to work at them to make them endure, and Dawn and Alyssa didn't seem like quitters. I thought they were meant to be, if only I could convince them of that.

"Who is moving, Dawn?" I asked. I knew the answer, but I needed a way to start the conversation.

"Alyssa has decided to move out. She can't bring herself to tell her parents about her sexuality, so she thinks it's best if we go our own ways," Dawn said, crying.

"I'm so sorry, Dawn, but maybe it's not over," I pointed out. "Maybe she just needs some more time to talk to her family. She can't deny her sexuality forever."

"You don't know her, really," Dawn said. "Alyssa can keep up appearances better than most. She's a very tough person, and she doesn't want anything to complicate her relationship with her family or her career."

"Sometimes a little space and time is good to clear your head," I replied. "The old saying, 'Absence makes the heart grow fonder,' isn't a thing for nothing. You're a special person, Dawn. Maybe she'll come to her senses when she realizes how much she misses you. A good jolt of the reality of being without you might be just what does the trick."

I hugged Dawn as she cried into my shoulder. Alyssa walked past us with a box in her hands. She did not look at me or Dawn. She was stoic and stiff. She looked like a woman on a mission, and I guess her mission was to pack up without engaging. This was a sorry scene indeed. I tried to stop Alyssa the second time she passed us, but she shrugged me off. It was clear I was intruding, and I couldn't make this better.

However, I meant what I said. Sometimes a little separation is a good thing. The distance might help Alyssa get the courage to talk to her parents after all. I know that may seem like wishful thinking on my part, but I'm an optimist through and through. Life throws you a lot of disappointments, so you can't let yourself get easily depressed or, worse, defeated.

After trying and failing to get Alyssa to stay, I went home. It was shaping up to be a horrible day. I was served a restraining order, the police had the wrong guy in custody, and my neighbors were breaking up. Some days are just all around bad, and this was one of those days for sure.

The good thing about bad days is they come to an end at some point, and better days are waiting just around the corner. That corner may seem far away, but you'll get there if you keep moving forward, and I surely was going to keep moving forward. Nobody was going to knock Sheila Sammartino off her game, at least not for too long.

When I got back in my house, I was greeted by stares from my mom, Tania, and Reggie. They were all waiting to hear that the killer, or at least one of them, had been caught. Unfortunately, I did not have any such news to share. My news was all bad. Everyone was disappointed to hear the wrong man was in custody, but we were all more determined than ever to find the right murderers. We had to see this through together.

"So Yolanda has flown the coop, and Shanice and Tom are giving each other a cover story," I said.

"We're going to solve this," said Momma. She could see I was feeling a bit down and needed a good cheering section. Momma was always the best cheering section for her kids.

"I don't see how we can pursue Yolanda when she is out of town," Tania noted.

"Let's think about what we want to find out about Yolanda. We want to know where her money is coming from and why she's selling properties," Reggie said.

"I agree, and we still want to find out more about her business relationship with Tom. Beyond the money, we can still pursue the emotional angle. If Tom and Shanice were getting together, they would surely want Arthur out of the way," I theorized. "I heard Arthur talking to Shanice, Yolanda, and a third person he was meeting at Harry's. I bet we could get a good lead out of knowing who that third person was."

"Also, all of this is assuming someone hired the two killers," Reggie said. "Maybe there is a way to finger the actual killers. We have to remember, they were the ones that committed the actual murder."

"I like the way you're thinking, Reggie," Momma chimed in. "The direct approach is often the best approach, in my opinion. If we find the murderers, we'll blow this whole situation wide open. We'll know everything, I'm sure of it."

This little brainstorming session was turning out to be very helpful. At least we were getting our thoughts out there. Sometimes it helps to just run ideas by your friends. Everyone needs a good sounding board every once in a while. We can't just depend on our own instincts to carry us through. As the proverb goes, it takes a village.

"I think we still have to look at Tom," Reggie said. "He has connections to Arthur, Yolanda, and Shanice. Yolanda or Shanice could have told him Arthur was at Harry's. Maybe he's the one that hired the killers. Yolanda was angered by what Arthur was up to, and she was Tom's partner, so he would want to keep her happy. He also wanted to be with Shanice. I think we have to look at Tom. Also, a closer look at him might reveal how Yolanda is getting funded."

"Yeah, but he has a restraining order on me. I can't go near him," I said.

"Maybe it doesn't have to be you," Tania interrupted. "Men relate best to other men. I think Reggie should give it a try."

"But he knows I'm with you guys," Reggie said.

"Nonsense, he just knows you're attached to Sheila somehow, so play that to your benefit. Maybe you tell him you were hanging around with Sheila to get a stake in her paper, but when she refused, you decided to go it alone. Now you're sticking it to Sheila and starting your own publication. Of course, that publication needs investors and a corporate headquarters. Pitch him on investing, and have him show you some office space. Maybe you can get another look at his books along the way."

"You are amazing, Tania!" I cried with joy.

"It's what I do," Tania said. "I always have a plan."

And it was a good plan. Reggie agreed to do it. He thought he could pull it off, so he quickly left to see if Tom would "work" with him. Through it all, Reggie had always been game to help us out and solve this murder. I know some people think concepts like fate are silly, but not me. I believe in fate. Some things just can't be explained, and they are just destined to happen, in my view.

When I hit Reggie with my car, it was one of the most embarrassing moments of my life. Imagine hitting your new neighbor as he moved in? You would be mortified too. Well, I was mortified for sure, but maybe it was also a turning point for me. Maybe I was destined to meet Reggie. I think some things are just meant to be.

Now it was just us ladies, Tania, Momma, and me. We had lots of work to do anyway. I started writing away and Tania started reading. Come hell or high water, we needed to get the publication out. There's a stigma that somehow online publications are lesser when compared to print, but it just isn't true. Most Americans get their news online, and my publication was a go-to place for many. Old-school folks like Lieutenant Crooks just don't understand the value of what I do. My online stories get more traction than the print stories I used to write, hands down.

"You ladies want something to eat while you work?" Momma asked.

"I will never turn that offer down," Tania replied.

So my momma went into the kitchen to busy herself cooking. My momma was the youngest of two. Aunt Ida was the eldest, so she did all the cooking. The eldest does everything while the young one gets away with everything. I should know, I'm the eldest and my brother, Johnnie, can do no wrong in my momma's eyes. So my momma didn't learn to cook until she got married. At that point, she had no choice, but she sure made up for lost time. She had her mom's recipes and perfected them. She also had tons of cookbooks all over the house. As I said, when my momma had a goal, she tackled it. Too bad she never perfected baking.

She whipped up some spaghetti and meatballs for us. Momma always made sure everyone was fed. You would never go hungry in our house growing up. Even after my dad left and my momma was working several jobs, she always made dinner. Talking around the dinner table was a must in our house.

She even gave some spaghetti to Majesta, who was very grateful. You could probably hear Majesta purring from next door. I had to admit, it was nice having Momma around.

"You girls still hungry?" she asked.

"I'm full, Momma Sue. That spaghetti and meatballs hit the spot," answered Tania.

"I'm good too, Momma," I said.

"What's going on at Dawn's place?" Momma asked.

"Do you remember Dawn?" I asked her.

"Of course I do. I remember all your neighbors from that wonderful dinner you invited me to a while back. Such nice people they are," Momma added.

"Dawn's girlfriend, Alyssa, is moving out. They got engaged, but they are having trouble. Relationships are tough. Alyssa has not come out to her family, and Dawn doesn't want to get married in secret," I reported.

"Surely, her parents have to know. Parents know these things. Our kids are our treasure. They are our prized possessions in life," Momma said.

"That's why I love you, Momma Sue. You're the best," Tania pointed out. The two hugged lovingly.

After that, my Momma waved her hand in the air to indicate that she remembered something. I asked where she was going. She said she had something in her bag she wanted to show me. She had just bought a gold bracelet. The bracelet had the infinity sign in the middle and hearts all around. The two closest hearts to the infinity sign had my name engraved on one and my brother's name engraved on the other.

"I just bought this to celebrate my love for you and your brother," she said.

My momma was very sentimental. It was a beautiful bracelet. It was heavy to the touch, and the gold was so yellow it picked up the light perfectly. I stared at it intently as my momma swirled it from side to side. In that moment, it picked up the light and nearly blinded me. All those hearts were flickering with light when I suddenly remembered what I saw in the alley when Arthur was killed.

"I can't believe I didn't put two and two together at the time," I said. "I pride myself on being so observant. I pride myself on being so inquisitive. Anyway, I remember an important clue now. I know where to find one of the murderers!"

CHAPTER 28
A PLAN TO CATCH A
MURDERER

I can't believe this didn't come to me sooner. Looking back on that day and what happened in my old newsroom, I should have thought of this sooner. Every year, my old boss Duke hosted an awards ceremony. He created a slate of journalism awards and gave them out each year. It was a black-tie event, and everyone was required to go. In his twisted mind, he felt like journalists would work harder if they knew they could get an award from him, but it really created a toxic culture. Everyone wanted to be recognized by him, so everyone wrote their stories in such a way that they would catch his eye.

It's not all bad to want to please the boss. Let's face it, everyone wants to be in their boss's good graces. That's only natural. However, as a journalist, I think there is a higher authority. What do I mean by that? Journalists are supposed to seek out truth. There's supposed to be a certain honor in journalism. Don't get me wrong, getting an award is great, but when that award is created and given out by one man, I think that's a problem. Who made Duke the authority on good journalism? Why wasn't there a board of judges? See what I mean here? The awards ended up being nothing more than a popularity contest designed to reward Duke's favorite employees.

Going into it, I knew I wasn't getting anything. He hated my brand of journalism, and he always told me so. Providing encouragement and dishing out constructive criticism was just not his style, and everyone knew it. The result was, you created a newsroom with two camps, the Duke kiss-ups, and those that didn't care at all about the awards. It was sad because if the award categories were crafted by a committee and the committee decided the winners, I think everyone would have been on board, and getting an award would have been a universally sought-after thing in the company.

Each year the gala ended with Duke giving out five awards. The event started with dinner and drinks and dancing. Think senior prom meets the Oscars. I liked the socializing because as a journalist, you are so focused on your stories and your deadlines that you don't always get a chance to really know all your colleagues.

The awards ceremony the second year I was with the company stood out to me because the first year, all five awards were given to men. The second year, one woman got an award. Her name was Sally Smith, but everyone called her Sally "Smarty Pants" Smith. Why? You can guess why. We all know people like Sally. She was self-absorbed and felt like she was always the smartest person in the room. Having a good sense of self is not all bad, but letting others know how wrong you think they are about pretty much everything—and how right you are about pretty much everything—is never a good look.

But I digress. The year she won stood out to me because of how Duke announced her. He called her "honey," and after handing her the award, he proceeded to slap her on the butt in front of everyone. You know what's worse? Nobody said a thing, and nobody seemed to even think anything was amiss or out of the ordinary about the behavior. Were we living in the Dark Ages? Come on, this was disrespectful and demeaning language and behavior.

I guess you also take your cue from the award recipient, and Sally "Smarty Pants" was all smiles. She got the award for writing a story about the Hearts. The Hearts are a local prostitution ring in town. Everyone knows they exist and what they do, and they're always in and out of jail. Well, Sally interviewed a bunch and did a piece on what it's like to be a Heart. It was a good piece, don't get me wrong, but

Sally being the author sat with me the wrong way. Also, it was heavy on cliches, and didn't do the girls justice, in my opinion. I guess that's why Duke loved it so much.

As Sally accepted her award, the smugness oozed out of her every pore. You could hear the conceit in her words and delivery. She was eating up the adulation. At the end of her speech, she showed off a gold charm bracelet filled with hearts and said wearing this bracelet was the calling card of the Hearts. It was like a nonsense show-and-tell moment, but again, Duke loved it.

Seeing the heart bracelet my momma bought just brought this whole episode back into my mind. I should have known earlier. I should have put two and two together sooner. I was kicking myself now. In that alley, when I saw them beating Arthur, I was blinded by the sun. Why? Because the light reflected off the female murderer's charm bracelet, which was filled with hearts. That woman was clearly a Heart. She was a local prostitute. I guess I was so distracted and overwhelmed in the moment, I didn't fully process everything, but this was literally staring me in the face. I remembered the bracelet, but it just didn't click with me until now what it meant. As the old saying goes, better late than never.

"What is it?" Momma asked.

"What do you mean?" I said.

"You are staring at my bracelet."

"I know those symbols. I've seen heart bracelets before. The female murderer was wearing one," I added.

"I can assure you, the murderer was not wearing this bracelet," Momma pointed out. Obviously, Momma spent a pretty penny on the bracelet. She was very proud of it. She wasn't going to have it soiled by a murderer. My momma was a very proud woman. Buying the bracelet was a very public way for her to show how important her children are to her, which is why it was so important for her to show it to me.

"Not that bracelet, Momma. I'm talking about a heart charm bracelet," I shared. Momma seemed to take a deep breath. She seemed almost relieved.

"What's the significance?" Tania asked.

"The heart bracelet means the female murderer is a Heart," I answered.

"What's a Heart?" asked Tania.

"Hearts are a local prostitution ring here. I remember a colleague reporting on them. She even got an award for her story," I reported. Momma's eyes widened and so did Tania's. I clearly got their attention. They were both paying close attention now.

"So we have to be prostitutes, I guess," Tania said.

"What?" Momma asked in shock.

"She means we need to go undercover as prostitutes," I translated.

"That sounds fun," Momma responded. My momma was up for anything, and she wasn't about to let us solve this murder without her. My momma had to be involved. The typical parent would warn about how this was a dangerous approach. She would probably discourage her child from even thinking about doing something so potentially dangerous. However, my momma was not normal. She was a can-do woman that would do rather than tell. Besides, she wasn't about to let me get into potential danger without the chance to protect me.

That summer Tania spent with us when she was on academic probation at school was a blast. My momma would go out with us. She would give us her take on the guys and keep us in line while also making sure we were always having a good time. That's just my momma for you. She hated drinking, but she never told us not to drink, just not to drink too much or get out of hand. Momma kept us in line without ever banning us from living life.

Tania, our resident planner, was very happy with the idea of us posing as prostitutes. She couldn't stop talking about it. Tania was almost giddy about it. She couldn't wait to get on the streets. It was a little weird, to be honest. Becoming a prostitute was not usually a person's first choice of occupations, and even posing as a prostitute wasn't exactly on most people's bucket lists of things they had to do in their lifetime. In fact, it was probably the last thing I wanted to do. But we were running out of leads, and we had to try something.

Reggie came back shortly thereafter from his visit with Tom. From the moment he came back, he was all smiles, so I knew things went very well. I guess they teach you in acting school to show your emotions on your face. I don't know for sure. I've never been to acting school, after all. But after observing how obvious Reggie's facial expressions and mannerisms were, my guess was he learned that in some school. It was obviously a learned behavior. I can't imagine anyone showing their emotions through a smile or a laugh as much as Reggie does. I have to admit, I think it's very cute and endearing.

"I've convinced Tom you are just obsessed with finding the truth about what happened to Arthur. I told him that's just how you are," Reggie said very proudly.

"I guess that's a compliment," I said.

"Of course it is, honey," Momma added. "Do you know any good reporter alive today that doesn't do that line of work because they want to seek out and report the truth?"

"Thank you, Momma," I noted. "However, not every reporter is so high-minded these days. It's a sad statement, but it's true."

"Anyway, we spent a lot of time talking about real estate. His first love is real estate. He just loves it. He loves buying and selling properties. He also manages properties and fixes them up. I decided not to go the route of telling him I wanted space to open a competing publication or making this a me versus Sheila thing. Like I said, I apologized on your behalf. I decided it would be a better approach to say I wanted to open a theater school for young kids. I think that's a better play for maybe getting him to drop the restraining order and getting some insight into his finances and, more importantly, Yolanda's finances," Reggie continued with vigor.

"I think that's a great idea," Tania replied. "You would be a great teacher and mentor. Any kid would be so lucky to learn how to act from you, Reggie."

You could tell Reggie was eating up the compliments. However, I have to say, they were not just meaningless words. I agreed 100 percent with Tania. Reggie is so supportive; he would be an amazing teacher.

I could sense Tania wanted to go further. She was eager to continue talking about playing prostitute. However, before those words could leave her mouth, I stepped on her toe, hard. She screamed in pain. Maybe I was too rough. Anyway, I didn't want her to get Reggie involved. We ladies could handle this while he dealt with Tom.

Reggie went on to explain he had a dinner set up with Tom to discuss the acting school further. He hoped to get Tom as an investor. Maybe at that point, he could get a better look at Tom's books and how he does business. Any insights would be helpful. We needed to know more about what made Tom tick and in turn, see what we could learn about Yolanda. I was not giving up on looking hard at Yolanda. No mother that lost her only child acts like Yolanda had throughout this ordeal.

Reggie left for his dinner, and Tania and Momma and I had to get into costume. We had to dress the part, after all. So we all went into my room to see what we could put together. It was easy to tell that Tania and Momma loved playing dress-up the way they delighted in going through my clothes.

"Why can't we tell Reggie?" asked Tania.

"Reggie has his own lead to follow. I don't want to distract him. If he knows what we are up to, he'll want to come along to protect us," I explained.

"Having a man around is not a bad thing, Sheila," Momma said. "Going on an adventure is also always worth doing, in my view. I always dreamed of travelling the world with your father after you and your brother left the house. Posing as a prostitute was not my idea of reaching that dream, but it's surely going to be an adventure, and the fact that I'm doing it with you girls means the world to me. Remember all those fun times we had the summer you stayed with us, Tania? Those were the days. We are going to catch this murderer tonight! I just know it!"

After "being" a prostitute for thirty minutes now, I can tell you it is not as action-packed as you might think. After getting all dolled up, we found a good corner and spotted a few ladies. We walked over to those working women and they just scurried. They walked away from us. There was literally no interaction at all. They stared us up and down and left. I was expecting more pushback for invading their space, or maybe more comradery for seeing new people on the block. Unfortunately, we just got nothing at all.

Fortunately, the next prostitute we ran into was more cooperative. Maybe it was because she was alone and not in a group. I think people are more likely to keep quiet when they are in groups. They don't want to be called out or singled out by their peers when they are saying something revealing or uncomfortable.

I looked down at her wrist right away. She did not have a heart bracelet, so she obviously was not a Heart; or maybe only some girls get the bracelet. Either way, she knew a lot about the Hearts. She gave us their usual locations. She wrote two addresses on a piece of paper for us.

Once she finished writing the second address, we heard the sirens. The police were following another girl they must have caught soliciting. The car was coming closer to us. The girl was running for her life right past us. What do we do? Tania started running, and Momma and I followed behind. Boy, am I out of shape! Running is hard. Maybe it's just running in heels that's hard. Either way, we ran for our lives. We were not going to get caught by the police and have to explain ourselves at the station. Lieutenant Crooks had too much fun serving me the restraining orders; this would make his day even more jubilant, and I was not going to let that happen.

Once we got back to our car, we started laughing. We all just started uncontrollably laughing. What was so funny? Nothing, really. I guess the thrill of getting away was so overwhelming, we just needed a release. We got away from the cops, and we got some solid leads as to where to find the Hearts; this was a pretty good outcome. We would have to come back out tomorrow night, which was a little disappointing, but regardless, our plan to catch the female murderer was really working. We were finally getting somewhere.

CHAPTER 29
STRENGTH IN NUMBERS

W ho knew how much fun it was going to be to run from the police? It was exhilarating, hightailing it back to the car. You watch all those cop shows, and you see the big, dramatic chases. It's a staple of those types of shows, really. Have you ever watched a cop show without a foot chase? Well, I guess there might be a few, but those are rare. You see the brave police officer running after the criminal all the time. They always run in the alley and get caught up when they encounter a chain fence, or sometimes they go up the fire escape and the whole thing unfolds on the roof. It's all rather predictable, but it still has a way of drawing you in and keeping you on the edge of your seat.

The other staple is the police officer is always very well put together. He's rarely overweight. It's like you must look like a Greek god to be a police officer in the movies or something.

The other commonality is they are usually men, as if you don't have women on the force. When Angie Dickinson premiered as Sergeant Pepper in 1974, it was considered groundbreaking. Really? Why is a woman playing a sergeant so groundbreaking? I guess it's not now, but back then, it certainly was.

In our case, we were the ones running from the police. Isn't that ironic? I'm a reporter trying to solve a murder and I end up running from the police. You would think the police would be grateful for the help, quite frankly. Regardless, it was a thrill, even if we were the "criminals" in this scenario. Thankfully, we got to our car and evaded arrest.

When I came down for breakfast the next morning, Momma was still excited about what we had done the night before. As they say, like mother, like daughter.

"Can you believe what we got ourselves into?" she asked with pride.

"I know, Momma. It was surely something," I replied. We were both a bit shocked about what happened, I have to admit, but getting out of it was such fun.

"The good news is, you got those addresses," she noted.

"Yup, we got some solid leads to follow. If we can find the actual killers, we can solve this case, even if it turns out to be a mugging gone wrong like the police seem so ready to believe."

It was nice to have a solid lead to follow up on. If we got to the actual murderers, that would be great. Following possible people that hired them just hadn't been working out for us. Let's face it, we'd gotten nowhere. Did I believe those murderers were hired? You bet. But following a more direct path and getting to the killers themselves might just be the way to go. Either way, we were going to solve this horrible murder and find out why poor Arthur met his end that morning in the alley.

When Tania arrived, she, too, was over the moon about last night, and she was more than ready for part two tonight.

"We got really far last night, but tonight we're going to get to the murderer. I know it," Tania said with certainty.

"At least we know where to find the Hearts," I said. It was important to keep the enthusiasm up. After all, what we were doing was dangerous, so we needed to stay super focused. We couldn't allow ourselves to be scared off or second-guess our plan; well, Tania's plan, to be exact. We were on to something solid.

The icing on the cake was that I was doing it with my best friend and my momma. It was a reminder of how close we are to each other and how lucky we are to have each other in our lives. So many people go through life without a clear support group, but not us. We were a great team, and that was something nobody could take away from us. Maybe that's why I didn't want Reggie involved in this one. He was following his own lead, and this gave us women a chance to do our own thing, which was very liberating.

Later that day, Reggie came to my house to report on how his dinner went with Tom. The great news was that he, too, felt like he made solid progress. Between our escapades with the prostitutes and Reggie's meeting with Tom, this investigation was going full force yet again. Reggie was happy he was contributing and, let's face it, he was a great addition to our little group of news sleuths.

"Everything went great with Tom. He likes the idea of creating a theater school for kids. I think he's going to invest in the project, and maybe, when he pulls the trigger, I can get more info on his finances and where Yolanda's money is coming from as well," Reggie said.

"I've said it several times now, Sheila, this one is a keeper," Momma said out loud. Reggie was quite impressed with himself. He was also very fond of my momma. I think hearing her compliment him was a good thing for his ego. Everyone needs a little self-esteem boost every now and then, and my momma was a pro at that.

In middle school, we had to memorize the fifty states and their capitals. It was excruciating. Momma and I studied together for weeks. I memorized more and more states and she quizzed me. Every day, the result of the quiz was a surprise. Some days I would do great, and other days I would fail miserably. Each night, Momma gave me more tips on how to be more consistently great, but I wasn't getting it.

The night before the actual exam, my momma sat me down. She said, "Sheila, you have studied so much. I don't know how things are going to go tomorrow, but you've done your best, and that's going to make everything okay in the end."

I scored a 90 on that exam. It wasn't 100, but that 90 was so hard-fought that it sure felt like I got 100. My momma put that test on our refrigerator and displayed it proudly. In my momma's eyes, you gained success by really trying and putting in all your effort, and who can argue with that?

Now Reggie was trying his best, and my momma was sure going to let him know it. Besides, I think she liked him anyway, and when Momma likes you, it's hard to do any wrong. My brother was always chasing the next quick fix, and she still propped him up and encouraged him as he switched to the next college major. It's just who she is.

"We've never really discussed your life, Reggie," Momma said.

"I'm an open book. What can I tell you?" Reggie responded. Tania and I watched intently. We both knew what was coming. Momma was about to grill him like a well-done hamburger.

"Are you married?" Momma asked.

"No, I am not married, and I've never been married. I guess I never found the right person," Reggie admitted. You could see a sense of disappointment in his face. Reggie clearly wanted companionship. I think he actually was longing for it.

"What about family?" Momma continued. She was not giving up until she knew everything there was to know about Reggie.

"I'm a twin, but my brother left the family after high school. He just wanted to go his own way, I guess. Both my parents are still alive and we're very close. I pursued a degree and a career in acting, but it never worked out, so I decided to write about theater instead. Sometimes things don't go as planned, but I don't believe in quitting. Dreams are meant to be achieved, even if life takes a different turn or two."

"Now that's a real man, Sheila," Momma said with zeal. She clearly liked Reggie's answers. He was winning her over with every new word. She looked me straight in the face in that moment but didn't say a word. She didn't have to. I knew what she was thinking. I knew what she'd been thinking since she first met Reggie. My momma was playing matchmaker in her own way, even if she didn't come out and say anything directly.

Tania interrupted the interrogation. "I'm glad things are going well with Tom, Reggie," she said. "We are doing great too."

Once again, I nudged her to keep quiet. This time, I pinched her arm. I think I was a little too rough because she screamed. Reggie looked confused. Any normal person would.

"I'm sorry, Tania, I just think we have lots more work to do on the paper and we need to get to it," I said.

"No worries, I'll let you guys get back to work. Tom is going to be showing me some locations for the performing arts space for the school, so I'll just be going," Reggie said as he got up to leave. I didn't walk him out because I was so focused on Tania, but once I heard the door close, I let her have it.

"I told you to keep things quiet! We are not going to tell Reggie we are posing as prostitutes to catch one of the killers. He would not think it was a good idea, and he'd try to involve himself to protect us, and we don't want that. We want to be free to see this through. And besides, he's busy with Tom!" I scolded her. "Now let's go upstairs and check out my closet again."

As we walked up to my room, I could have sworn I heard a door closing. I went to the front door, but nobody was there. I guess it was just my imagination or something. I'd been meaning to change this front door forever. It's not well insulated, and I don't really like how it looks either. It's old and worn. I always dreamed of having a house with a fancy, red front door, but red is a very loud color, so I don't think it will ever happen.

Tonight we knew we were going to be with and among the Hearts, so we decided to park a bit further away. We didn't want to be seen next to the car. Besides, the walking was good for everyone. We saw the ladies from a distance. They stood so straight. The women we met the night before were not as confident. These women were a special breed, and they knew it. Maybe being a Heart requires a certain self-awareness, who knows. I guess this line of work requires a certain demeanor. A Heart must act and behave a certain way, and they seemed to know it. Hopefully, that wasn't going to complicate our purpose for being there, but we'd soon find out.

We got right up to them and they instinctively started to circle us. They didn't run away or walk off. Their eyes were set on us. They were inspecting us from head to toe as they continued circling. It was quite intimidating. I couldn't spot any lady with platinum-blonde hair and pink tips, though. To be sure, their hair colors were very vibrant, but nothing like what I saw on the woman in the alley when Arthur was killed.

"Who are you?" asked what seemed to be the lead Heart. She had dark-black hair with bright-purple streaks.

"We're new here, but we hear you guys are the ones to know," I replied.

"Darling, you're nothing if you don't know us," another Heart said. This one had bright-orange hair and a funny laugh. She seemed like she was gasping for air when she laughed. Maybe she was a smoker or something. That would make sense. They all seemed a bit high on something.

"We are actually looking for one of your friends," Momma said.

"We don't have friends," the lead Heart replied.

"Of course, we're not friends either; I meant coworkers," Momma answered. She was very proud of her retort, but it did not impress the Hearts at all. This was going downhill fast. I had to step in.

"What she meant to say was, we're looking for a blonde with pink tips. Do you know someone with platinum hair and pink tips?" I asked.

"Why?" the Heart with orange hair asked.

"We saw her a while back and we owe her a favor," Tania interrupted. "I don't like owing anyone, so I want to pay up."

This amused the Hearts. They seemed to understand Tania's point of view. I think it struck a chord with them.

"I know what you mean. We must stick together out here, but we also have to make our own way on these streets. I might be able to help you," the Heart with purple highlights noted.

Perfect! Now we were going to get everything we needed. We were going to meet one of the murderers. It was finally going to happen.

"Run!" another girl yelled from around the corner. "The cops!" I looked up. It was her.

In that moment, everyone scattered, and we could now hear the sirens. The timing could not have been worse. The Hearts split up and went in several directions. I guess the thinking was the police would have to choose which one to follow if they scattered, which would increase their chances of not getting a trip to the station.

Of course, Tania, Momma, and I stuck together, but we ran all the same. One of the cops got back in their car now, and they were coming for us. You know how I said running from the police last night was exhilarating? Well, I was wrong to say that. Running from the police is just stressful, to say the least.

As we rounded a corner, Momma tripped. She busted her heel. Tania and I stopped to pick her up. Thankfully, she wasn't hurt, but the police car was getting closer and closer. We were in for it. We were going to get caught.

Just as I was ready to throw in the towel, a car pulled up and the driver swung open the door. All three of us looked in the familiar car. It was Reggie.

"Get in!" he screamed at us. We packed in his car quickly and the police drove by. Thankfully, we were undetected. Reggie saved us for sure.

"We're all part of this team, ladies," he said encouragingly. He was happy to be there to help, but also wanted to make it clear that the next time we did something dangerous, he was going to be right there with us. "I can't believe you would do this without telling me. Don't you know there's strength in numbers?"

CHAPTER 30
MONEY TALKS

My heart was pounding like a drum. I did want to do this with Tania and Momma but, boy, I was relieved to see Reggie. I wondered how he knew where we were. He was obviously following us, but he was supposed to be meeting Tom to see some properties this evening, so something must have gone wrong somewhere. My guess was that Tom got wise to what we were doing. He must have discovered that Reggie was just playing him for information. What else could it be?

"Great to see you ladies," Reggie said sarcastically. "I love the new wardrobe. You guys sure know how to dress up."

"We can explain," Tania said.

"Why do we have to explain?" I asked. "Reggie should explain why he's here and not with Tom."

"I knew you three were hiding something, so I pretended to leave your house earlier. Nobody got up to show me out, so I just closed the door and didn't leave. Instead, I did some snooping on you three. I heard everything about your little plan and rushed out of the house for real as you all went upstairs to get your clothes together," Reggie said with an air of arrogance. He was very proud of himself. He got to rescue us, and he was loving every minute of it.

"That's why I heard the door close a second time," I said. I couldn't believe he tricked us.

"Exactly," Reggie replied. "Now tell me what you guys found."

"Wait, what about your meeting with Tom?" I asked.

"After overhearing your little plan, I called Tom and asked if he could show me the properties tomorrow. I figured my time was better spent here, and I guess I was right," Reggie pointed out. Reggie was right. We needed his help. It was a good thing he overheard us after all. He was right, there is strength in numbers, especially when you're posing as a prostitute. Everyone needs a helping hand sometimes. I was just grateful Reggie was there to help us out.

"Thank you," I said.

"Let's face it, ever since you hit me with your car, I haven't been able to let you out of my sight," Reggie openly admitted. "I just can't imagine us not doing this together."

"What else are you imagining when it comes to Sheila?" Tania joked. My momma smacked her gently but firmly.

"I've been waiting a long time for this, let the man continue," Momma said.

"I think I said what I had to say, Momma Sue," Reggie replied with a smile. "The rest is up to your daughter."

"Well, not to change the topic, but to change the topic, we found one of the murderers tonight," I interrupted. "Unfortunately, the police spotted us, so everyone ran for it. But we're getting close."

"Your problem is that, number one, you're too conspicuous, and number two, you don't have a lookout. We'll come back tomorrow night and I'll stay in the car and act as your lookout. If the police come, I'll try to distract them so you can have more time talking with your new coworkers," Reggie plotted.

"Good plan," Tania commented.

So we called it a night. It was a good plan. Maybe I should have included Reggie in our little plan after all. I was wrong to exclude him. We needed Reggie on board. *I* needed Reggie on board.

The next morning began with an interrogation from my momma. She was not happy with how I left things in the car with Reggie, and she was going to let me know it. My momma was a woman of very few words, and I was about to get a few of those choice words unleashed on me. She meant well, but remaining silent or in the background was just not her style. When my momma had something on her mind, she was going to share it, no matter if you liked to hear it or not.

"You left that man hanging last night," she scolded.

"What are you talking about?" I asked. I knew exactly what she was talking about, but I am more comfortable asking the questions compared with answering them. Besides, this was a question I wanted to outright ignore. How could I talk to her about my feelings for Reggie when I was so confused about how I felt and how he felt? What did he want from me anyway? Did he want a girlfriend or just a section in my publication?

"That man is interested in you, and I think you're interested in him too," Momma pointed out. Every mother wants their daughter settled, and my momma was no exception to that rule. I couldn't blame her for what she was trying to encourage here.

"We'll see how it goes," I answered.

"What do you mean, young lady? Men don't wait around forever," Momma pointed out. She was right again. Reggie was not going to wait around, and it wasn't fair of me to make him. He obviously wanted me to make the first move. Some guys are like that. They don't want to be let down. Let's face it, nobody likes to be let down. I was just going to have to consider my situation and come to some decision about what I wanted to do. Easy, right? More like easier said than done.

Fortunately for me, the doorbell rang. I didn't want to continue this conversation with Momma, and I was clearly saved by Tania. However, it was a bit early for Tania to show up for work. Maybe she was in an ambitious mood today.

Nope, this was not Tania at all. I couldn't believe who it was. It was Shanice. Why would she be here at my house?

"Can I come in, please?" Shanice asked.

"You have a restraining order on me; we can't be this close. I don't want any trouble," I said.

"We've dropped the restraining order. Tom and I both dropped the restraining orders. I'm here to clear the air with you," Shanice reported.

I welcomed her in. I welcomed everything about her news, in fact. Nobody wants a restraining order put on them. It was a big weight lifted, knowing I no longer had two on me.

"Tom and I are getting married. We want a fresh start. The morning Arthur was murdered, Tom was with me. After the call you overheard between Arthur and me, we were together. I went to see him, and he was in his office. Arthur knew things were over. I had no reason to kill him or hire anyone to kill him. When it comes to Tom, he and Yolanda are doing very well financially. Tom had no reason to kill him either."

Shanice placed two pieces of paper in front of me. I picked them up. One was her phone bill and the other was a note. "What's this?" I asked.

"One is my phone bill and the other is a note I got from Yolanda that she sent to me with instructions to give it to you. Tom and I just want to put this whole thing behind us. If I was talking to Tom right after I talked to Arthur that morning, he could not have been the murderer. Now, if you'll excuse me, I have a date with my fiancé."

Shanice left, confident I wouldn't bother her again. I was eager for her to go. I wanted to read the note from Yolanda. What could she possibly have to say to me? The note read:

Dear Sheila,

I hope all is well with you. All is well with me. I'm getting some needed rest and relaxation. I know you're trying to help my son by finding who's responsible for his death. I hope this little quote helps you on your quest:

"All we've been through, for nothing but an idea! Something that you cannot taste, smell, or feel; without substance, life, reality, memory. Power corrupts."

What the heck did that mean? What was I supposed to learn from this cryptic letter and philosophical quote? She was obviously trying to tell me something. Yolanda was always secretive. She was never straightforward, but this took the cake. She wanted me to solve this murder with a quote? I was never going to figure this one out on my own.

I looked at the phone bill, and everything Shanice said was corroborated there in black and white. I showed Tania everything when she got in. She didn't know what to make of Yolanda's note. She was just as confused as I was about everything.

Momma went through everything also. She was stumped as well. Surely, if the three of us could not figure out the note, nobody could. This was a dead end for sure. This note meant nothing at all. It was just a way for a manipulative woman to manipulate more people. That's just what Yolanda was good at.

Reggie stopped by later. I tried to show him the note, but he had some news of his own he was eager to share.

"I have some good news and some not so good news," he said. "Tom and Shanice are getting married, and they've dropped the restraining orders on you, Sheila."

"We know, Shanice dropped by earlier," I shared. "What's the bad news?"

"Tom doesn't want to invest in the theater school for kids," Reggie pointed out. "So I don't think I'm going to get a look at his books. He's happy to show me more properties if I want to go it alone. He'll help me find the office space I would need, but that's it."

"We ran into our own dead end. Shanice shared her phone bill with me. She was talking to Tom when Arthur was killed. She also gave me this note from Yolanda, but I can't make anything of it. I don't think it means anything," I said as I handed it to Reggie. He read it quickly and his eyes widened.

"This is easy. It's a quote from *Camelot*. King Arthur is reflecting on his failed ambitions. But the last part about power corrupting is added. That wasn't in the musical," Reggie reported.

"Of course, Yolanda was obsessed with Camelot. That's how Arthur got his name. But why would she add that part about corruption to it?" I wondered out loud.

"We can't let this distract us. Let's keep this in the back of our minds, but without any more solid leads, we have to find that murderer tonight," Tania said. She was right, of course. The pressure was on for this next meeting with the Hearts to produce something concrete. We needed real answers.

It was easy to find the Hearts this time around. We knew where to look, and they stood out quite a bit. Fortunately, it seemed to be the same group from last night. Walking the streets at night surely is dangerous, but doing it with Reggie did make me feel much safer this time around. Not that I need a man to protect me or anything, but having one around was very handy, I must admit. Besides, Reggie brought a lot to the table. His flair for the dramatic and his willingness to help when needed have been invaluable assets.

Reggie waited in the car as we three approached the Hearts again. They remembered us, clearly, and just like last night, they quickly started circling. This must be their go-to method of approach.

"We're back," I said.

"We wish you'd just go away. I talked to Pixie. You don't owe her anything. She doesn't know you," said the Heart with the purple highlights in her hair.

"Is her name Pixie?" Momma asked. "What's her last name?"

"You ask too many questions," the lead Heart responded. "People who ask too many questions get hurt! We've had enough of you three."

Well, this wasn't going well. The lead Heart pushed Momma. Pushing Momma was never a good idea, though. My momma slapped her hard, so hard she fell to the ground. Before you knew it, we were in a brawl. They were tugging at our clothes, and we were fighting back ferociously. We were not going to be intimidated.

However, it didn't last long. Reggie got out of the car and quickly broke everything up. He got in the middle of everyone and the scuffle was ended.

"Now, let's not fight, ladies," he said.

"Who are you?" the lead Heart asked.

"I'm about to be your best friend. Let's spend some time together. Would you follow me in the car for a little meeting?" Reggie noted.

The lead Heart was interested. Reggie showed her a few hundred-dollar bills and she followed him willingly into the car. They talked for a few minutes. It seemed like they were having a real in-depth conversation. Reggie knew what he was doing. Within twenty minutes the meeting was over and she left the car.

Reggie came out of the car and waved us over to come with him. We all crowded back in Reggie's car.

"I know where your murderer is," he said with glee. "That Heart was happy to tell me everything I wanted to know. Money talks, after all. Now, let's catch a murderer."

CHAPTER 31
WE ARE TOO LATE

Thankfully, we brought a bunch of makeup remover. Once we got in the car, I started removing the caked-on makeup. It's just not me. I'm a simple person. I don't wear much makeup, and my clothes are, well, simple too. Also, I work from my home, so I don't really have to impress. In addition, I'm the boss, so that helps.

Tania still dresses very nicely each day. She looks like she could be going to the office. That's just not my style. Certainly, all this makeup was not my style. Taking it off was very liberating, in fact. I felt more like me without it.

Now that we were done posing as prostitutes, it wasn't needed, so why keep it on a second longer than I needed to? I was ready to get to this location and meet this murderer, who would undoubtedly reveal the second murderer when cornered, and we'd finally have our answers.

"You are amazing!" Momma said to Reggie.

"Well, you know, I try my best," Reggie replied. Once again, Momma's compliments were going straight to his head.

"So where are we going?" I asked.

"Violet told me Pixie is meeting a regular client at this hotel," Reggie shared. He handed me a piece of paper with the name and the address of the hotel. "Her client set up the meeting with her yesterday. She was told to meet him there."

"Who's Violet?" I asked.

"Oh, that's the Heart I talked to with the purple streaks in her hair. That's what she calls herself. Appropriate, isn't it?" Reggie noted. He was on a roll and he knew it. He might have literally just broken this case right open.

"Why was the meeting set up in advance?" I pressed Reggie. I was sure he didn't ask all the right questions. He's not a reporter like me, but I must see what he found out.

"Actually, the client called her to set up the meeting because she told the client she might be pregnant. As it turns out, Pixie—that's your murderer's name, by the way—has been seeing a few very high-profile clients regularly and just recently discovered she might be with child. She doesn't know who the father is for sure, but she suspects this guy she's seeing now may be the daddy. Every time you think this is going to be straightforward, it just gets more convoluted. But when you think about it, life is never a straight line, there are always twists and turns," Reggie said very philosophically. Make no mistake, Reggie was no philosopher, but he was very introspective and thoughtful, so his insights about how he views life made a lot of sense given what I'd observed about him.

"Damn straight," Momma said. "You never know what life is going to throw your way, but having a partner there to help you along sure does help." Momma looked at me intently. I knew what she was getting at without saying a word. Her meaning was crystal clear; at least, to me it was crystal clear. She wasn't going to come out and ask Reggie out for me, but she was going to keep pushing me to make that move until maybe, I listened to her.

We pulled up to the hotel. It was more like a dive. Your typical cheap motel. The sign in the front was neon, but half the letters were dark because not all the lights were working. It was called The Lounge. What a sophisticated name for such a low-class place. My guess was that most of the guests weren't coming here to lounge; quite the opposite.

Tonight, things were not popping. I didn't see a single car. The

Lounge was deserted. Maybe everyone was still out and about, but it was late at night. You would think people would already be here doing whatever they usually did here.

"You need someone to stay in the car and keep watch," Momma said, rightly so. "Tania and I will stay here while you and Reggie talk to the manager and find that Pixie girl."

"I want to come too," Tania moaned. She sounded like a child that had not gotten their way. Momma put her arm on Tania's shoulder and gave her a cold look.

"Nonsense, I'm getting old. I need Tania to stay behind with me. You two go ahead and take your time," Momma said with conviction. Tania did not argue. As she knew well, there really wasn't much point in arguing with Momma.

I have to admit, I am not accustomed to spending time at these types of motels. It's a bit scary, really. The silver lining was the fact that it was so quiet and still. You could hear everything and, thankfully, there wasn't much to hear. I looked around and did see a few lights on in some of the rooms. It wasn't much, mind you, but there were two or three rooms with their lights on. I wasn't sure if that made me feel safer or more cautious. The more people in a place like this, the more chance of uncovering all kinds of debauchery.

We made it to the front desk. Nobody was visible except a few roaches that scattered once we entered. That wasn't the type of greeting I was hoping for, but it wasn't unexpected. We rang the bell at the front desk and the manager quickly came out to greet us. Now that's the greeting I was hoping for.

"How can I help you folks?" he asked.

"We're looking for a girl with platinum-blonde hair and pink tips," Reggie said.

"Are you police?" the manager asked with a twinge of fear in his voice. I guessed he was used to getting visits from the police, and they were not too pleasant.

"No, she's a friend," I said.

"In that case, she's in room number two. She's a sweet girl. She comes here often," the manager said.

"Does she meet people here that you've seen?" I asked.

"I don't know. She's always the only one that comes here to get the key. Maybe she tells her friends the room number after she gets the key from me? I don't know, really. I don't leave this office. You never know what's out there. I stay right here and she's the only one I ever see; she's always by herself, and I like it that way, if you know what I mean," the manager admitted candidly. I could see where he was coming from. I wouldn't want to leave the front desk either if I were him.

We walked slowly over to room two. I looked back at the car. I could see Momma and Tania. They were staring at us. Momma started waving. I brought it to Reggie's attention. He waved back and laughed. I must admit, it was funny to see her waving so vigorously. I laughed a bit as well. The anticipation was building. I could feel the proverbial lump in my throat as we got closer and closer to the room. What would she say when confronted? Why was Arthur killed? Did she even know Arthur? Questions like this and many more were swirling around in my head.

Once we got to the door, we just looked at each other. Reggie also realized the sheer gravity of what we were doing. I wondered if he had a lump in his throat like I did. Was he scared? He seemed calm enough, and quite put together. Reggie was ready to knock on the door so I motioned my head, giving approval.

He knocked, but nobody answered. The thumping on the door seemed so loud in comparison to the total silence around us in that moment. Reggie knocked again, but there still was no answer.

"Just here to check the air-conditioning!" Reggie shouted. I guessed maybe he thought posing as some kind of repair person might get her to come to the door. Quite frankly, I wasn't convinced this place even had air-conditioning. It was a good try, but nobody answered the door. Pixie was either sleeping or otherwise indisposed. I didn't hear any noises coming from inside the room at all. We were surrounded by the darkness of the night and the stillness of the motel. Nothing was moving.

So I knocked on the door myself. No response. I knocked harder. Still no response. The third knock was so hard, the door itself opened. I guessed it was slightly ajar and we didn't even notice. Who could blame us under those circumstances?

With the door fully open now, we walked into the room. The lights were off. It was just as dark inside as it was outside; in fact, I think it was darker inside the room. Reggie turned the light on and I screamed at what I saw in front of me. There was Pixie on the bed, lying there, dead. The platinum-blonde hair and pink tips were plain to see. This was the female murderer I saw. I was sure of it. Blood was coming down the side of her face. She had been shot in the head. Reggie ran over to her and saw a gun on the floor right next to the bed.

How could this be? We were so close. If we were here even a bit sooner maybe, we could have saved her. Despite all our best efforts, we were just too late.

CHAPTER 32
NOW WHAT?

Thankfully, Lieutenant Crooks was not the officer that came to The Lounge Motel when we called 9-1-1. I don't know if I could have dealt with him right about then. I'd gone from leading a normal life to now seeing two dead bodies. My guess was that Pixie was also murdered, just like Arthur. But with so few people in the motel and the manager not seeing who she met there, I wasn't sure anyone truly witnessed what happened to her. At least the police couldn't call this one a mugging. Who would mug a prostitute in a dive motel? Nobody, that's who.

As I looked at her dead body, I wondered what brought her to this point. Why did she become a prostitute? Why was she in this motel? Who was she meeting? You know me by now, always thinking and questioning. It's what I do. It's my nature. Her right arm was outstretched, and the gun was on the floor right below it. It seemed so weird to me that she would fall on the bed that way. It almost looks staged to look as if she fainted and fell back on the bed in true dramatic form.

Reggie was looking around too. "Does that seem like a fake pose to you?" he asked.

"I was thinking the same thing," I replied.

Then, a police officer came out from the bathroom holding a piece of paper. "You're going to want to see this," the police officer said to his partner. "I think our victim committed suicide. She left a note."

"That can't be right," I said.

"Please leave this to the police," the other officer said. "We'll take it from here."

Where have I heard that before? Lieutenant Crooks wasn't here, but maybe this guy was channeling him or something.

Momma and Tania ran into the room after that. The three of us shared a big hug. Reggie was not included. It was a girl thing. We were bonding over a shared sense of grief like only a mother and child and best friend could.

"What happened, Sheila?" Momma asked.

"Who are these people?" one of the officers asked.

"This is my momma and my best friend," I explained.

"This is not a slumber party, ladies. We're going to ask everyone to go home. My partner has your information, so we'll call with further questions," the officer instructed.

We left the room and went back to the car. Now was a perfect time for us to regroup.

"What do we do now?" Momma asked.

"We could go back to ask that Heart with the purple hair if she knew any of Pixie's clients," said Tania.

"That Heart is called Violet. That's not a bad idea. We asked the manager here that question before going in the room. He had no idea who Pixie met here, but she was a regular," Reggie noted. Thankfully, all four of us had our wits about us. None of us were too overwhelmed to really think this through.

"Maybe, but I have another idea that might get us some actual answers. I think we should find out more about Pixie. I'm going to go to the police station in the morning and talk to Anthony. Maybe she has a police record. He'll know and he'll tell me," I said. Reggie seemed upset by my comment, but he didn't say anything.

The next morning, Momma was up early. That meant she had something to say to me that she was stewing over. Maybe she wanted to talk about the murder. I doubted that was it, though. I was pretty sure it was another matter entirely.

"Did you sleep well, Sheila?" she asked.

"Yes, I did, Momma. What about you?" I replied.

"I made you some coffee and blueberry muffins. Well, the blueberry muffins were in your pantry, but I warmed them up for you."

"Thanks, Momma. What's up?"

"I think we need to talk, sweetie," she said seriously. Clearly, the small talk was over, and she was ready to come to the point. "What are you going to do about Reggie, honestly?"

"What do you mean?" I asked. I knew perfectly well what she meant, but I wasn't about to admit it.

"He likes you and you like him, so give him a chance. He's been by your side this whole time, honey," Momma noted. She was right, of course. Reggie had been invaluable.

"Like I told you, he hasn't really talked to me about those types of feelings," I answered honestly.

"Why do you think that is? Is it possibly because you fawn over Anthony all the time and he doesn't want to be your second choice if you have your heart set on Anthony?"

That was a keen observation. I never thought of it that way. Maybe Reggie thought I had feelings for Anthony and it was stopping him from being clearer with me about his feelings for me. "I'll think about it, Momma, but right now, I'm off to see if I can ask Anthony a few questions about Pixie. I'll see you later."

Anthony was not hard to spot. He was near the watercooler, wrapped around another lady. This one had dark-black hair and enchanting, green eyes. It was easy to see why Anthony was drawn to her. She looked all smiles from here. She was obviously into him too. I walked right over to greet the two of them

"Why is it, every time I come to talk to you, I see you talking to a different woman?" I asked Anthony.

"I'm just friendly, I guess," he responded. He thought he was cute, but his female companion was not impressed. She left without saying a word.

"I'm so sorry to break up your little talk," I said.

"No worries, I'll get to her again later," Anthony confided. "What can I do for you?"

I told him about how we tracked down and found Pixie dead last night. Anthony was not surprised. He knew who Pixie was, and I guess the thought of me finding a dead person was common at this point, as well.

"She's a frequent flyer here. I know her well," Anthony shared. "What do you need from me?"

"Was she ever arrested?" I asked.

"Many times, but she never got convicted of anything. Everyone here was convinced she was born under a lucky star or something," Anthony laughed.

"Can you make a copy of her record and share it with me?" I begged like a cute little puppy. He placed his finger over his mouth as if to motion me to keep quiet. He walked over to the files, made a few copies, and gave them to me. Before I could thank him, he again put his finger over his mouth and walked away.

I got what I came for and I was going to get out while I was ahead. Unfortunately, I wasn't so lucky. I was stopped by Lieutenant Crooks. He was very eager to talk to me, which meant nothing but bad news for me.

"It's been a while, Sheila," he said.

"Yes, but it hasn't been long enough, actually," I replied sarcastically.

"I'm glad your mother is not here with you. That woman is scary," he pointed out. "I just wanted to make sure you were not going to be involving yourself in another one of our cases."

"Now that those restraining orders you delivered have been lifted, I'm pretty footloose and fancy-free. Who knows what I'll do or where I'll go," I noted with a smile.

"I just wanted to let you know face-to-face that I heard about your encounter last night at The Lounge. We found a suicide note and we're ruling it, you guessed it, a suicide," he reported. He was very clear and direct in his delivery. This was a warning to me that I should leave this alone.

"You can't do that!" I yelled at him. "This was no suicide, and after I talk to a few people, I'll prove it!"

I guess I was loud because DA Clarence Wright came over. I could see him hovering in the background, but I wasn't sure if he was focused on me or someone else at the time. He walked over to me and Crooks and put his hand on my shoulder.

"What seems to be the problem here? Everyone is staring at you two," he pointed out. I looked around and he was right. I was so focused on Crooks, I didn't even notice.

"I'm sorry, sir. I have some things to tend to," Crooks said before walking away.

I had to admit seeing him walk away was very satisfying. Anytime Crooks is put in his place, it's a good time, as far as I'm concerned.

"What's this I hear about you and a prostitute?" Clarence asked.

"We found her dead. She was murdered," I said. Crooks wasn't going to listen to me, but maybe Clarence would. He was always self-absorbed, but he always struck me as family-oriented; after all, his campaign for governor centered on family values, so I respected him for that.

"I heard it was a suicide," Clarence said.

"I don't think so. I talked to one of her friends, and she seemed to think Pixie was pregnant and had a meeting with one of the possible daddies," I shared.

"Oh my God, do you believe that?" Clarence asked.

"I don't know what to believe," I answered, exasperated. These past few days were taking a toll on me. "Arthur's death is still a big mystery, and now this. What do I do now? I have to figure it out."

"What you need is a little break," Clarence said. "I'm giving a big speech tomorrow. I want you to come."

"I'm not really a political person," I admitted.

"You're a reporter, and reporters love a scoop. I'm going to have some big policy news, and if you come to the speech, I'll give you an exclusive interview afterwards. It'll be fun, and it'll get your mind off this stuff for a while. What do you say? I'll have my assistant email you all the details. Will you be there?"

"Actually, that might be a great change of pace. Of course I'll be there," I said. Clarence was right, it would be nice to get a scoop and report on something new and fresh. What could go wrong?

CHAPTER 33
A DEADLY ENCOUNTER

The house was quiet today. Tania and I were working in the living room, and Momma was cooking, of course. The great thing about having Tania and Momma both around was that the conversation never stopped. The two fed off each other. They always had something to say about literally everything. Just yesterday, they had an hour-long conversation about the rug in my living room. Both women agreed it had to be changed, but the style of the new rug was in dispute. Tania favored a more modern look, while Momma favored smaller throw rugs placed strategically throughout the room.

Today, however, conversation wasn't flowing, about the rug or anything else. When I saw Arthur murdered, everyone rallied around me, but this time, we all saw a dead body, which made it different, I guess. We were all shaken at the same time, so there was nobody to act as our cheering section this time around.

Even my cat, Majesta, was quiet. She was off in her favorite corner of the room giving herself a nice bath.

Well, it was up to someone to break the silence and bring us back to the world of the living, and being that nobody else seemed willing or capable, I guessed it was my job to get this group back on track.

"Look, people, what happened last night was horrible, but we all know it wasn't a suicide," I said as Momma came in the room with a batch of croissants.

"How do we know that?" Momma asked.

"If Pixie thought she was pregnant, would she kill herself? And right when she had a meeting with the man she thought was the father?" I pressed. It just didn't make sense to me. The timing was all wrong.

"Maybe the baby daddy rejected her and she couldn't take it," Tania said.

"I guess that's possible, but those Hearts had so much attitude. I find it hard to believe she'd crumble like that. Also, getting pregnant is not exactly unexpected in their line of work. Mistakes happen," I added.

Momma and Tania were both nodding their heads in agreement. I had struck a chord with them. They knew I was onto something. I couldn't help thinking that Arthur's murder and Pixie's murder were connected.

"What if the person that hired Pixie and the other guy to kill Arthur was feeling the heat and needed to get her out of the way?" I thought out loud. "After all, Pixie would have no reason to be involved in Arthur's murder unless she was working with someone. Maybe the guy with the beard is pulling all the strings, or maybe someone else hired both of them."

Before Tania or Momma could chime in, the doorbell rang. It was Reggie. I was so happy to see him. He always brightened the outlook in the room. He always made me smile.

"Are you ready?" he asked.

"Ready for what?" I responded. I was confused. Was something happening I forgot about?

"You have to get to Clarence's rally for that exclusive interview he promised you," Reggie reported.

"You're right, I totally forgot about that!" I responded. What kind of reporter forgets about an exclusive? I'd just been so distracted.

Momma came to the door to see who I was talking to. Once she saw Reggie, she smiled. I guessed he had a similar effect on her too.

"What brings you here, dear?" she asked.

"I came to escort Sheila to Clarence's rally. He promised her an exclusive interview," Reggie noted.

"Who's at the door?" Tania asked as she, too, walked over.

Before you knew it, all four of us were crowded near the door. It was a silly sight when we had a whole house to go in. Why converse at the door when there are comfortable sofas to sit on? We were a crazy bunch, for sure, but that's what made us special.

"He's here to take Sheila out," Momma said, smiling.

"He's here to take me to the rally, Momma," I corrected.

"Of course," she replied. "I think it's best if you two go and Tania and I will hold down the fort here."

"But I want to go to the rally," Tania begged. Momma stepped on her foot and Tania screamed. Now she saw what Momma was trying to accomplish here. "Oh, okay, we'll stay here."

"You two have fun," Momma said with glee as she pushed us out the door and closed it shut. That was our cue to be off to the rally.

I was sure it was by design that Clarence was giving this speech in Unity Park. The park holds special meaning for our town of Harmony. It used to be open space filled with grass and trees. People congregated there, but it was very forest-like. So our mayor decided to make a change. They built a man-made lake, a big gazebo, jogging trails, and a playground for kids. After all the work was done, they had a big ribbon-cutting ceremony and named it Unity Park.

In the end, the park did bring the community together, as intended. It's a wonderful place to hang out and have a picnic or just curl up on one of the benches with a good book. The park is surrounded on all sides by residential buildings, so it was really a great location to get a lot of our residents out of their homes and into the fresh air.

Clarence was using the gazebo for his speech. He was going to be talking from the gazebo out to his crowd, which I was sure was intentional. He wanted a big, local crowd there cheering him on. It'd make the local news, and I was sure it would get coverage throughout the state as well.

You have to hand it to politicians; they know how to set a scene, deliver a speech, and get as much attention as possible.

I thought this was the first time Reggie visited Unity Park since moving next door, so I was excited to be the one to show him around. I'm no tour guide or resident town historian, but I knew enough to talk about the history of the place without coming across as foolish. At least I hoped I wouldn't come across as foolish. I wanted to show Reggie a good time. He deserved it for all the help and support he'd given me.

As soon as we arrived, we saw a relatively big crowd around the gazebo. Clarence obviously did a good job of getting the word out. Also, Harmony is a very proud place, so the idea of cheering on a local guy as he tries to be the next governor is certainly a draw. Harmony residents support other Harmony residents, and I don't think anyone from Harmony has ever run for statewide office, so this was a welcome first for us.

Once we walked over to the spot of the speech, we were greeted by Anthony. Maybe he was there on behalf of the police to oversee security, or maybe he was just curious to see what Clarence was set to talk about, but either way, he was there, and he walked over to us once he saw me.

"Hello, Sheila," Anthony said. "What brings you here? I didn't think politics was your thing."

"Not usually, but Clarence offered me an exclusive after the speech. He said I had to come, so I'm here. What reporter doesn't like an exclusive?" I noted.

"I'll let you guys socialize," Reggie said. He started to walk away, but I stopped him. I grabbed him by the arm and turned him around to face me.

"Nonsense, I'm here with you," I said to Reggie. He was clearly very happy with that comment because he proceeded to hold me close as Clarence began to speak. I looked over at him a few times and I could see he was smiling.

"This country is based on family values," Clarence said with conviction. "Hard-working families are the backbone of America. How do I know that? I come from one of those families. My father was a hard-working immigrant that became who he was because of the goodness of America. He often compared our great country to an onion. He said it's dark and ugly when you first see it, with all the skin and stuff, but once you peel back the layers, you see a beautiful, yellowish center that makes any meal taste simply amazing. My father was right! He passed away recently, but my campaign will keep his spirit alive! I'm going to be a governor for every family in this state. I'm going to be a governor that launches policies to make sure every family can succeed, just like my family has."

I had to hand it to Clarence; he is a great speaker. I also liked that little story about his father. It sounded so familiar to me, I was sure I'd heard him tell it to me before. When you remember family stories of the DA, you know you're spending too much time at the police station. I needed to get out more, for sure. Reggie was paying close attention to Clarence, but I could see he was having a good time.

All was right with the world until I felt something hard in my back. It was like someone was shoving a piece of metal in my spine. It hurt! I turned around to see the bearded man right behind me. He looked down at his right hand as if to tell me to look there too. He was holding a gun, and he was pointing it straight at me. He lifted his finger to his mouth to indicate I should keep quiet, and he discreetly motioned the gun as if to tell me to walk off with him. What should I do? I wasn't going to leave with him! This man was a murderer! It takes a lot of guts to pull a gun on someone in a crowd, but I guessed that was the plan because everyone was so focused on Clarence's speech, they were not paying too much attention to the crowd.

No matter, I wasn't going to end up like Arthur or Pixie, so I screamed: "No!"

Reggie, who was standing right next to me, quickly turned and saw the gun. He took action. He punched the guy straight in the nose and hard, too. The bearded man fell back a few steps, and now everyone was looking at him.

He quickly gained his footing and started to run toward one of the residential buildings. He was determined not to get caught, and I guessed he wanted me dead. He must have recognized me in that alley after all, but he didn't plan on me having a guest with me like Reggie.

"That's the man I saw murder Arthur!" I yelled.

Reggie and I ran after him, but after Anthony heard me yelling, he, too, followed quickly behind us. Pretty soon the three of us were all running after the bearded man. We followed him into an alley between two of the residential buildings. He turned for a second and fired at us, but the bullet didn't hit any of us. The man was frantic, and just shot in our general direction. This guy was not a professional killer, and he was clearly terrified.

At the end of the alley, there was nothing but a chain-link fence. He was trapped and he knew it, so he decided to climb up the fire escape to the roof, and all three of us followed behind him. Just like on TV.

Soon, we all got to the roof. I wasn't sure what I planned to do once I caught up to him. Reggie and I didn't have a gun, and this guy clearly did, but we weren't going to let him get away, regardless. I didn't think this through at all, but thankfully, Anthony was there, and he had his gun drawn. Anthony was ready for this guy.

"Let's just calm down," Anthony said to the man. "Whatever is going on here, it doesn't have to escalate."

"You don't know me!" the bearded man shouted back. "You don't know where I come from! My brother went to jail, and he came back a changed man! He told me stories! I will do whatever I have to do to avoid that!"

After making that declaration, he turned away from us and started running really fast. This man was clearly out of his league. Where was he going to go? Then I realized what he was doing. He was going to try and jump from one residential building to the next to get away. That was crazy! These buildings were too far apart! He'd never make it! But that didn't stop him from trying. He leaped…and fell.

Reggie, Anthony, and I ran to the edge of the roof and looked down. The bearded man was down below on the concrete pavement, dead.

CHAPTER 34
SECRETS REVEALED

Now we were down on the pavement next to the bearded man's body. There were police everywhere. It was an active crime scene. Thankfully, we had a police officer with us the whole time, so we didn't have to stay around too long. After all our searching, sleuthing, and snooping, we found both of Arthur's murderers, and when we did, they both ended up dead themselves.

I couldn't help feeling uneasy, though. I was still not clear on how they knew Arthur, and why this guy turned on Pixie. So many unanswered questions remained. Anthony came over to chat with me as I continued to ponder what just happened.

"Are you okay, Sheila?" he asked.

"Yup, I'm okay," I answered. "That is definitely the man I saw murder Arthur in the alley, and the prostitute from the other night was his partner, I guess."

"Mystery solved," Anthony said with glee.

"But why did they do it, and why did this guy also kill Pixie?" I wondered out loud.

"Who knows? Maybe it was a mugging gone wrong after all. Either way, one of the guys has identified your bearded man. He said he was in and out of the station on several burglary charges and con schemes.

Clarence could never make anything stick though," Anthony reported. "We'll be done questioning your friend Reggie in a bit. You two should go home."

As if on cue, Clarence entered the alley. He looked very concerned. This whole situation ruined his speech. I was sure he'd worked very hard on the buildup and delivery of that talk only to have it ruined by this murderer. I was sure he was quite pissed off right now.

"I'm sorry this had to happen to you," Clarence said. "I've obviously got to find another way to finish that speech of mine too. This guy sure knows how to crash an event. What can we do? At least you didn't get hurt and it's all over."

"I don't know if it is, Clarence. He's the guy I saw murder Arthur. He must have murdered Pixie also, but why?" I asked Clarence.

"That's horrible, but at least this is behind you now," Clarence noted.

"I don't think it is. I have to know why," I said. I looked over at the dead body and thought to myself, I am not going to let this go until I have all the answers. I just can't. Then I looked up at Clarence, who was staring at me sympathetically.

"I think you should go home and get some rest, then stop by my office after hours tonight at nine p.m. Everyone will be gone by then. I'll give you that scoop I promised, and this day will end as it should," Clarence said.

I agreed. Reggie walked over. The police were done with him, so we went home and told Tania and Momma what happened. It was a crazy day. We agreed to meet back up tomorrow at my house to discuss next steps. That left me and Momma to prepare dinner. It had been nice to have dinner with Momma these past few days.

Just as we were about to sit down at the table, the doorbell rang. It was Dawn. She had been crying. I invited her in, and once Momma saw her, she ran to her and gave her a big hug.

"I remember you, dear," said Momma. "Tell Momma why you're upset."

The three of us sat down in the living room. I was sure things with Alyssa were not getting any better. Poor Dawn. Things don't always work out. I knew that all too well, having been through what I'd been through. Every time I thought we were onto something with this murder, more questions came up in my head. It was really maddening and, given my determination to know everything, just made the whole matter even worse.

"I really thought Alyssa was the one," Dawn said.

"She was a very nice person. I think we all enjoyed having her on the block, but not everything works out as we plan," I said.

"Nonsense!" Momma asserted with conviction. "Who taught you to give up like that, Sheila? You listen to Momma, Dawn. Do you love that girl?"

"Yes, I do," Dawn replied.

"In that case, you need to fight for her. You need to call her and tell her how you feel. Don't give up just yet," Momma advised.

"Well, I haven't talked to her since she moved out," Dawn remembered.

"There you go," Momma pointed out. "You need to go home and call her."

Dawn was encouraged. Momma said all the right things. Momma always said all the right things. Dawn marched out of my house as if she was on a mission. Hopefully, it would all work out well for her.

Dinner was wonderful! Momma and I had a great time together. After that, we sat on the sofa before I had to leave to meet Clarence. I was surely going to get that scoop Clarence promised me. This day was going to end well, with me at least getting a good story to tell my readers tomorrow.

"You see, Momma knows best," she said to me.

"You are the best, Momma," I said as we hugged.

"Now that Dawn has listened to me, it's your turn, Sheila," Momma said to me.

"What advice do you have for me?" I asked. I knew what was coming, and I was ready to hear it again. Even Majesta jumped on the coffee table to listen to Momma. She was on a roll, and she knew it. She had everyone's attention, just how she liked it. Momma was ready to make a point, and she wanted everyone listening—well, at least me and Majesta.

"You'd better not let that neighbor of yours get away from you,

Sheila. He's a good man, and you can use a good man in your life," Momma pointed out.

"I know, Momma, but I've never been great at relationships, you know that," I admitted.

"That's your problem, Sheila! You don't listen! You need to take a lesson from Dawn and listen to what I'm telling you!" Momma said with feeling.

I looked down in shame and I saw Majesta on the table sitting on a bunch of papers. One of the papers was the copy of Pixie's police record Anthony had made for me. *It can't be. I think I see it now!* I grabbed the copy and looked closer.

"Momma, you're right! I have to listen more!" I said to her as I got to my feet. I remembered it all. Everything I was told, it all made sense now. I just wasn't listening, and this police report confirmed it. "I know what happened! I've figured it out! I need to call Reggie and Anthony on my way to see Clarence. I have tasks for them. Momma, you are amazing, as always!"

I raced to the police station, and in what seemed like no time, I was at the door to Clarence's office. I walked in proudly and he was sitting behind his desk, expecting me.

"I'm here for my scoop, Clarence. I want you to confess to making Pixie and that bearded man murder Arthur and then getting rid of Pixie after that," I said to him. I thought he would be shocked, but he wasn't shocked at all. He seemed almost like he was expecting me to say what I did.

"You always did have an overactive imagination," Clarence said. "Why would I have anyone murdered?"

"Arthur is your half-brother, and he was blackmailing you. He called the third person I overheard him talking to 'bro.' I thought it was slang at the time, but it wasn't. You two were brothers. You couldn't have it get out in the press that you had a long-lost, illegitimate half-brother. And to top it all off, he was Black, also. You were not going to risk this news crippling your election, so you called on two cronies to kill him for you. You would continue to keep Pixie and the bearded man out of jail if they did you this one favor: murder Arthur," I revealed to him.

"How could you know Arthur was my half-brother?" Clarence asked.

"I finally listened. When my Momma said I should listen more to what people tell me, I remembered the story you told about your father comparing America to an onion. It was so eloquent. I knew I'd heard that story before. I thought I heard it from you, but then I remembered I heard it from Eugenia. You probably don't know Eugenia, but she is Yolanda's friend. Yolanda never told her who Arthur's father was, but she told Eugenia Arthur's father was a hard-working immigrant that often compared our country to an onion. She had to be talking about your father. Who else would think to make that comparison?

"Yolanda was getting money from your father, which she was using to buy properties and create wealth for herself. When I was leaning on her too much, she must have called you to get her out of the country. She wanted to keep everything quiet, which is why she didn't like that her son was getting involved with you. However, she had no idea what you did to her son until we saw that bearded man deliver the money and plane tickets. I told her at the airport the bearded man was the one I saw murder her son, and that's when she knew. On her 'vacation,' she sent me a letter about power corrupting. I didn't get it at first, but I do now. She was pointing me to you. She believed your quest to be governor had corrupted you to get rid of Arthur, and she was right."

"Even if this is true, why would I murder the prostitute?" Clarence asked.

"We found out the prostitute was pregnant and had a meeting set up at The Lounge with the baby's father. My guess is, that was you," I reported to him. "You must have been seeing Pixie on the side. Who knows if you really were the father, but you couldn't chance it, so you told the bearded man to murder her and make it look like a suicide. It was also no coincidence that the bearded man tried to kill me at your rally, because you invited me to the rally when I told you I knew Pixie was pregnant and I wasn't going to stop looking into things. He didn't recognize me from the alley at all, you sent him to murder me."

"You can't prove any of this!" Clarence bellowed.

"I have Yolanda's note, and I think it will be easy to track your father's money into her accounts now that we know what we're looking for. All I have to do is go public with the story; and I have a lot of reporter friends that will help me get it out there, given my background, of course.

"In terms of proving you murdered Pixie, I noticed your name was all over her police report. It's no coincidence that every time she was brought in, you took the case and lost it. I noticed that as I was looking at her police record. My guess is the same pattern will show up in the bearded man's record too. Also, I have Reggie circulating your picture among Pixie's prostitute friends right now. I'm sure someone will remember seeing you with Pixie."

My cell phone text notification chimed. It was Reggie, as if on cue. "Just as I suspected. I have my next-door neighbor showing your picture to Pixie's friends that we met on the streets. You were cautious, but two girls have said they saw you with Pixie. I think their testimony will prove very damaging, don't you?"

"You're too smart for your own good. I tried to convince you to leave this alone several times, but you wouldn't listen," Clarence said. He pulled a gun out of his top drawer and pointed it at me. "I thought borrowing the police uniforms and the squad car would give them cover when they got Arthur. I thought they would just drop his dead body off in the alley. I didn't expect they'd kill him in the alley.

"You did get one thing wrong about Arthur though, he was not blackmailing me, really. He wanted to reconnect, and he wanted me to give him a job in my campaign. He was trying to establish a relationship with me and use me to get himself a new job and a new life. I couldn't have that. Who knows when it would have turned into blackmail? I'm going to be governor, and nobody is going to stop me. I had to get rid of him.

You are one hundred percent right about the prostitute, though. She said I was the father of her baby. How does she know? She probably sees hundreds of guys. It didn't matter, I couldn't let that get out, so she had to go too. Now it's your turn to go, and if I have to take care of your friend Reggie, I'll take care of him also."

"Now, Anthony!" I yelled.

Clarence was shocked as the front door to his office swung open and there was Anthony with his gun drawn.

"It's over, Clarence," he said.

"You didn't think I'd come here alone, did you? Oh, and by the way, I'm a reporter, so I had my audio recorder in my pocket the whole time, taping our conversation."

Clarence was caught and he knew it. He dropped the gun and Anthony took him out of the office in handcuffs. Finally, it all made sense, and Arthur could truly rest in peace. His murder was solved, and Clarence was going to jail.

CHAPTER 35
NEW BEGINNINGS

I t was that time again. Everyone on the block was getting together for our dinner. This time, it was at my house. But given all the recent activity, I decided to have it catered, with Harry's help, of course. All of this started when I saw Arthur's murder outside his deli. Who could imagine I'd witness a murder after eating his amazing bagels that morning? Certainly, not me.

Momma was excited to see all my neighbors before she left. It was time for her to go home. She felt good knowing she was there for me throughout this ordeal, but it was time for her to go back to her big house in Swanky-ville, and she realized it. Momma always knows best.

"I've had so much fun here with you, Sheila," she said. "It's been a great visit. Admit that it's been a great visit."

"It has been a great visit, Momma," I said lovingly.

But once she realized I was having the dinner catered, she quickly became critical. Harry set the food up on the table and she inspected everything. Momma was brutal as she walked around and around the table. She was like a drill sergeant or something. She was also very free with the insults. This was not going to be good.

"This food looks wonderful, but surely you could have had me cook," she said. "Everyone knows I can cook better than this. I'm an amazing cook. You've even told me so many times, Sheila."

"How dare you insult my food?" Harry said in anger. He was a sweet man, but his pride was hurt. Harry loved his food. "You haven't even tasted it! I assure you, it is amazing! Your daughter loves my cooking!"

"It looks okay, I guess," Momma said, which angered Harry even more. Momma had clearly stepped over a line with Harry.

"You don't know what you are talking about!" Harry shouted as he stomped out of the house.

"That wasn't very nice, Momma," I said.

It took Momma a while to responded. She was clearly distracted. She was thinking hard about something, I could tell. In true Momma form, it wasn't long before she revealed what was on her mind. She can't hold anything in.

"He's kind of cute. I think I'll be visiting more often, Sheila," Momma explained as she smiled from ear to ear.

Soon after that, all the neighbors arrived, and we were so excited to see each other. Everyone was catching up and talking about the murder. They were thankful it was over, and everything turned out okay in the end. Who doesn't love a happy ending, after all? As we all sat down at the table to eat, the doorbell rang. Who was that? Everyone was already here.

I opened the door, and it was Alyssa. It worked! Dawn must have called, and here Alyssa was.

"I hope there's room for me," Alyssa said.

"There's always room for you," I replied.

I grabbed Alyssa by the arm and rushed her into the dining room. Once Dawn saw her, she rose to her feet while everyone stared in silence.

"I got your voicemail. I was wrong. I want to move back in. I want to get married, if you'll have me," Alyssa said.

"Of course I'll have you," Dawn responded. She quickly ran over to Alyssa and there was a lot of hugging and a lot of crying. Everyone crowded around the two of them to congratulate them. Momma was right. Dawn listened to Momma, and it all turned out just right. Now it was my turn to listen to Momma. So I tapped Reggie on the shoulder and told him I wanted to speak to him in the other room.

"Is everything okay?" he asked.

"Everything is perfect. You're perfect," I told Reggie. "You've been amazing this whole time, and I've been thinking. I think my publication needs an entertainment section after all, and I'd like you to be the one to write it. I think we have a lot more to do together."

"I thought you'd never ask," he said with glee. "Of course I'll write it, and I agree, we do have a lot more to do together."

I looked up at my bookshelf to see the magnifying glass my old boss Charlie gave me. He told me to remember to always look deeper and ask questions when he gave me that memento. I keep it next to my laptop up there. Charlie was right. I saw what I saw, an innocent man was murdered, and I could not stand by as the police tried to minimize it.

Now the murder is solved, and I look at Reggie and see more. I see my possible future. I grabbed his hand and squeezed it affectionately. We walked back into the dining room together. What a wonderful night this was!

EPILOGUE

You won't believe what happens next … Watch for Book 2 in
The Harmony Neighborhood Cozy Mystery Series "A
Twisted Engagement" by Tony Garritano.

After Sheila solved the murder of Arthur Jones, you would think
that life in Harmony would return to normal. However, the usual
harmony in Harmony is short lived, at least for Sheila and her neighbors, Dawn and Alyssa.

The couple comes out to Alyssa's family and announce their
engagement. The response is not favorable, but eventually fences are
mended. To make up for their initial displeasure, Alyssa's family
decide to throw the couple an engagement party. Most engagement
parties are joyous occasions, but this one turns deadly when a guest is
found stabbed and Dawn is accused of the murder.

Of course, Sheila believes that her friend is innocent, but the police
are convinced that Dawn is the murderer. So, Sheila, her copy editor
Tania, and her new entertainment writer Reggie set out to prove her
innocence. What they uncover is a twisted story filled with many
secrets and lies.

ABOUT THE AUTHOR

Tony Garritano was raised by a single mom that made him who he is today. Now he lives in a small town in Connecticut with his best friend/wife, two sons, mother-in-law, two cats and two dogs. Tony enjoys cartooning, Star Trek and quiet time with his family, pets and a good book. As a child, he grew up dreaming of being a mystery writer. Today that dream is a reality. Winner of Four OUTSTANDING CREATOR BOOK AWARDS; the LITERARY TITAN BOOK AWARD; the MAINCREST MEDIA BOOK AWARD for Mystery/Suspense; the FIREBIRD BOOK AWARD for Suspense; and the INDIES TODAY BOOK AWARD, his first book "I Saw What I Saw: A Harmony Neighborhood Cozy Mystery" is a huge success. All the books in the Harmony Neighborhood Cozy Mystery Series can be found on Amazon.

Made in United States
North Haven, CT
19 November 2022

26909219R10133